John Peel is the author of numerous best-selling novels for young adults, including installments in the *Star Trek*, *Are You Afraid of the Dark?* and *Where in the World Is Carmen Sandiego?* series. He is also the author of many acclaimed novels of science fiction, horror, and suspense.

Mr. Peel currently lives on the outer rim of the Diadem, on a planet popularly known as Earth.

BOOK OF
DOOM

John Peel

Llewellyn Publications
Woodbury, Minnesota

First Llewellyn Edition
First printing, 2005

Book design by Andrew Karre & Megan Attwood
Cover design by Gavin Dayton Duffy
Cover illustration ©2005 Bleu Turrell/Artworks   FR
Editing by Rhiannon Ross

Llewellyn is a registered trademark of Llewellyn Worldwide, Ltd.

Library of Congress Cataloging-in-Publication Data
Peel, John, 1954–
Book of Doom / by John Peel.
     p. cm.—(Diadem, Worlds of Magic; #10)
Summary: In the continuing adventures of Score, Helaine, Pixel, and Jenna, they find that Pixel is possessed by Nantor, his evil "other" self, which causes an imbalance of the magic throughout the Diadem.
ISBN-13: 978-0-7387-0842-3
ISBN-10: 0-7387-0842-9
[1. Magic—Fiction. 2. Good and evil—Fiction. 3. Friendship—Fiction. 4. Fantasy.] I. Title
PZ7.P348Bh 2006
[Fic]—dc22

Llewellyn Worldwide does not participate in, endorse, or have any authority or responsibility concerning private business transactions between our authors and the public.
     All mail addressed to the author is forwarded but the publisher cannot, unless specifically instructed by the author, give out an address or phone number.

Llewellyn Publications
A Division of Llewellyn Worldwide, Ltd.
2143 Wooddale Drive, Dept. 0-7387-0842-9
Woodbury, MN 55125-2989, U.S.A.
www.llewellyn.com

Printed in the United States of America

For Rochelle and Crystal Beiersdorfer

PROLOGUE

"This is very disturbing," Shanara announced. "I wish I knew what was going on!" She paced back and forward across her room, chewing on her lower lip. From his perch on the table, Blink opened one eye and looked at her.

"You should learn to relax more," he informed her. "Am I worried? No. I wait, and see what will happen when it reveals itself."

"Relax?" Shanara whirled around in mid-pace, her long lime-green hair spinning about her beautiful face. "How *can* I relax? Magic has started to break down. Oracle has been missing for hours, and I can't work a spell to find out what's happened to Score, Helaine, Pixel, and Jenna. Everything is breaking down, and all you can suggest is that I try and relax? Are you insane?"

"No." The red panda stretched, yawned, and then tried to settle back to sleep. "I know my limitations, and I feel the best thing I can do is conserve my energy for when it's most needed. You should also. All that pacing of yours makes me exhausted just to watch."

"You're not watching," Shanara growled. "Your eyes are closed."

"Well, I can *hear* you," Blink grumbled. "Can't you fret and panic quietly?"

Shanara glared at him. She was about to say something when she felt a shimmering in the air. "At last!" she exclaimed, as Oracle reappeared. "Where have you been for so long?"

Oracle sighed. He was a tall man, dressed entirely in black, though quite elegantly. Shanara could vaguely see through him because he wasn't completely

" Shanara whirled around in mid-pace, her
-green hair spinning about her beautiful
v can I relax? Magic has started to break
cle has been missing for hours, and I can't
ell to find out what's happened to Score,
Pixel, and Jenna. Everything is breaking
all you can suggest is that I try and relax?
sane?"

he red panda stretched, yawned, and then
ttle back to sleep. "I know my limitations,
he best thing I can do is conserve my en-
hen it's most needed. You should also. All
g of yours makes me exhausted just to

ot watching," Shanara growled. "Your eyes

can *hear* you," Blink grumbled. "Can't you
hic quietly?"
glared at him. She was about to say some-
she felt a shimmering in the air. "At last!"
hed, as Oracle reappeared. "Where have
r so long?"
ghed. He was a tall man, dressed entirely
hough quite elegantly. Shanara could
through him because he wasn't completely

For Rochelle and Crystal Beiersdorfer

P

Shana
what
and f
on he
table
at he
"Y
infor
wait
reve

"Relax?
long lime
face. "Hov
down. Ora
work a sp
Helaine,
down, and
Are you in
"No." T
tried to se
and I feel
ergy for wl
that pacin
watch."
"You're
are closed.'
"Well, I
fret and pa
Shanara
thing when
she exclai
you been fo
Oracle si
in black,
vaguely see

real—he was a magical construct, an image of a man. As a result, he could be wherever he chose, and was able to walk between worlds, and to go to places too dangerous for a person who had a solid body that could be harmed. Three hours ago, he had left her to journey to the world of Jewel. Jewel lay at the heart of the Diadem, and was the place where magic was the strongest. It was so strong that if she ever visited it, the power would burn her body up. Few living beings could ever go there, but it was perfectly safe for Oracle.

"Troubles rage and problems breed,
This is the hour of greatest need."

Shanara stared at Oracle in horror. "You're still talking in rhyme," she gasped. "Has magic broken down that far?" The flow of magic in the Diadem was controlled from Jewel. She had felt that there was a breakdown, which was why Oracle had been there to investigate. In the heart of Jewel was a special room. Inside it was a magical analog of the Diadem, where each world was represented by a jewel, and inside each jewel a spirit from that world was held captive. As long as the analog worked, magic was intact.

"Our plight is bad and getting worse,
The problem now we can't reverse.

Our only chance that I can find
Is to set the trap we have in mind."

"The trap?" Shanara felt a chill sweep through her. She and Oracle had indeed been preparing a trap, one that both had sincerely hoped would never be needed. The Diadem analog had been maintained by Score, Helaine, and Pixel, who had siphoned off some of their own power to keep it going. The room had then been sealed by a unicorn's horn, which negated all magic that approached it. Nobody but Oracle or one of the three young magicians could enter that room. Shanara and Oracle had been afraid that the analog was breaking down when the flow of magic had become damaged. "What has happened to the analog?" she demanded. She knew she was avoiding the subject of their trap.

"The analog is breaking here.
The problem is on Calomir.
The jewel that held grim Nantor's soul,
Is empty now, and growing cold."

Nantor! Shanara gasped. The three youngsters she had befriended and helped had turned out to be not quite what they seemed. The Diadem had once been mercilessly controlled by the Three Who Rule—Nantor, Eremin, and Traxis. They had been attacked, and had vanished—only to reappear as their own younger selves. Score, Helaine, and Pixel were not exactly the tyrannical Traxis, Eremin, and Nantor, but they all had the potential to grow into those cold, heartless villains. Shanara had grown to know and love the three youngsters—and Jenna, who had later joined them—and had felt almost certain that they could never become the Three again. But . . . it was that "almost" that had scared her.

She and Oracle knew that they could never take the chance that the Three might return. If they did, the Diadem would be plunged back into abject slavery and misery. So they had prepared a trap, just in case—a trap that even the great powers of Pixel, Score, and Helaine couldn't defeat. Shanara had felt as if she was betraying the youngsters even by planning the trap, and she had prayed desperately that it would never need to be used.

But now Oracle was saying that they had no other option. They had to spring the trap that was meant to kill the three young magicians . . .

"Do we have to?" Shanara asked, so softly her voice was almost lost.

"To save the worlds we have no choice.

You must give the magics voice.

Prepare the trap, all set to fall—
Or else it's ruin for us all."

Shanara knew there were tears running down her cheeks, but she didn't care. To kill her friends . . . ! But Oracle was right—if Nantor had escaped somehow, then it would only be a short while before that evil genius found a way to free his two partners in terror. And once all three were free, the Diadem would be doomed. There was no choice in the matter—it was better by far that her friends should die than to allow the enslavement of countless worlds.

Shanara nodded slowly, grimly. "Alright," she agreed, her voice choking in her throat. "As you say, we have no choice. The Three Who Rule cannot be allowed to go free. I shall prepare the trap." She shuddered. "My poor young friends . . ."

"I too shall mourn when they are gone.
But this is our task, and must be done."

Shanara nodded, and turned back to Blink, who had fallen asleep again. "Awake, you lazy beast!" she cried, funneling her grief into anger at him. "This is a time of great danger—and great betrayal. It is not the time to sleep!"

Blink shivered, and opened one eye to look at her. "Now what's going on?" he complained. "I know that there's a great disaster, but does it have to spoil my rest?"

"Yes." Shanara began preparing for the spell they must cast. She needed Blink's help, because this was the strongest and most terrible spell she had ever made.

It was a spell to kill Score, Helaine, and Pixel . . .

1

Score stared at the
boy who had been
one of his best friends, and realized that
he no longer knew him. Pixel—the gentle, geeky, blue-skinned, pointy-eared
guy—still looked as he always had, but
now he was inhabited by a malevolent
entity—Nantor.

Dayta, the very cute blue-skinned,
pointy-eared girl who had somehow
latched onto them, was completely
confused, of course. She looked from
"Pixel," to Score, to Helaine, and then

to Jenna, who was still wincing from the magical blows she'd taken while trying to greet Pixel. "What's he talking about?" she asked.

Score didn't know how to handle the situation yet. Nantor only had the same power level that he, Helaine, and Jenna possessed—but he had a thousand years of extra experience in using magic. Maybe the three of them acting together could take him out— but that was by no means certain. And Jenna was weak right now. The best thing to do was to stall, and hope that one of them came up with an idea—and that it wasn't Nantor who achieved it first.

"Pixel has been possessed, in a sense," Score explained. "A possible future self, one he might grow into, has taken over. One that's evil, corrupt, and totally selfish."

Nantor smiled nastily. "And you forgot to add *all-powerful*," he pointed out.

"You're not all-powerful," Helaine growled. "Not without the other two members of the Three Who Rule, and you won't ever get them back."

Nantor laughed. "And who can stop me?" he asked, waving his hand at them. "You? Four children?" He made a sudden lunge and gripped Dayta's face. She gasped. "And this one can't even do magic!" He shoved her aside, ignoring her squeal of pain as she fell to the floor. "You other three know I have more magic than the three of you combined."

"Yeah, right," Score sneered. "That's why you're trying to talk us to death. And you're forgetting two important things."

Nantor raised an eyebrow. "Oh? Really? And what might they be?"

"First," Score pointed out, "the fact that however you managed to free yourself, it's upset the balance of magic in the Diadem again. So even if you have great magical skills, they're just as likely to go screwy as any. Magic has become unpredictable and unstable again."

"Only until I restore the balance," Nantor said, dismissing the problem. "And that will happen just as soon as I replace your feeble minds with those of Eremin and Traxis."

"Oh, *that's* a good plan," Score sneered. "In case you've suffered major memory loss during your time imprisoned in the mystical gemstone, the last time you and those two losers tried working together you argued so much that you managed to get yourselves deposed as supreme tyrants and jammed into gems. So do you *really* think that bringing those bozos back is a clever move?"

"I've learned from my past mistakes," Nantor answered. "This time, we *will* do better, because we have seen the consequences of failure. Once the Three Who Rule are restored, there will be stability for the Diadem again."

Jenna shook her head. "*Your* idea of stability," she pointed out. "Where you three rule, and everyone else is your slave."

"Of course." Nantor seemed amused. "You're too new to this magic business to understand the rules, but here's your first, last, and only lesson: power is for those who have it. Everyone else bows down to it, or dies. It's very simple, little girl." He moved over to her. "I have to say, Pixel did have *some* taste. You're rather pretty, in a common sort of way. Maybe I'll make you my queen—until I get bored with you, of course."

Score grinned to himself. "Are you sure Eremin won't get jealous? She's not the sort to share anything—or anyone."

"Eremin will have no say in the matter," Nantor said, sharply.

"Ooh, problems already, and she's not even back yet." Score shook his head. "Like I said, not a smart move, aiming to bring her back. And there's still the second thing you've forgotten about, you know."

"Oh, yes, your feeble attempts to distract me." Nantor smiled evilly. "And what's the second thing I've neglected?"

"The Overmind," Score replied.

Nantor glanced at the blank screen on the far wall. "That moronic computer?" he asked, puzzled. "It does not even comprehend magic; it can do nothing to interfere with my plans."

Score was more than half-afraid that Nantor was right, but he was certain that Nantor was overlooking a lot. "Your problem is that you don't understand science," he explained. "The Overmind hasn't been defeated—and if it's retreated elsewhere, then it's up to something. Probably just waiting for a chance to get you while your back is turned." Score really hoped that he wasn't just making this up. But when he and the others had entered the building, it had been deserted. He hadn't understood where all of the people had gone, but he was starting to get the glimmerings of an idea. This was the headquarters of the Overmind, and the staff here were probably absolutely essential to him. The Overmind was a living computer program, which controlled humans through microchips placed in their heads. It needed people as its hands, so if it was planning a counter-attack against Nantor, it would most likely remove its people from the building first.

Which meant that it might not be very long before it launched some sort of attack . . . And that didn't give him, Helaine, and Jenna much time to defeat Nantor first. Assuming that they *could* defeat Nantor . . .

Nantor looked smug as he shook his head. "I'm not worried about that computer," he said. "In fact, I need it to help me in my plans. What I need next is to have it install chips into you and Helaine. That will give Traxis and Eremin their chance to invade your brains and take them over, as I did with Pixel."

Helaine shook her head. "Do you think for one second that I would *ever* allow Eremin into my soul?" she asked. "I loathe her more than any being."

"She is you, you fool," Nantor growled. "You—once you realize what the true nature of power is."

"She is a cold, heartless bitch," Helaine replied, almost spitting. "And I will *never* become her."

"Of course she won't," Score agreed. "Helaine's such a warm, fuzzy, fun-loving gal that she could never turn into someone repressed, unemotional and who loves killing. Oh, wait . . ."

As he had expected, Helaine looked as if he'd just slapped her across the face. She whirled angrily to scream something, which was precisely the distraction he'd been hoping for. While Nantor was watching, amused, Score fired off two spells, and prayed that they would both work perfectly—not guaranteed, considering the way magic was starting to get screwed up.

The first one kind of worked—he'd attempted to throw a huge fireball at Nantor, while the magician was unprepared for an attack. Instead of a fireball, though, he shot off what looked more like a feeble marble of flames. Nantor was certainly taken by surprise, but he swatted the blast aside without any real effort.

"Do you imagine you can challenge *me?*" he exclaimed. "You're even more demented than Pixel's memories tell me."

Jenna latched onto that. "So Pixel is still alive!"

"Alive?" Nantor shook his head. "Only if you think being kept caged in a small portion of this brain is *alive*. And he won't last long. I'll worm him out of there and destroy him."

But there was now hope in Jenna's face, and Score knew he felt something of the same. He'd been trying to ignore his fear that Pixel was dead, and now he no longer had to. Pixel was still alive, and that meant there was a chance he could be restored somehow to controlling his own mind again.

But, meanwhile, he was in serious trouble. Score could feel the magic gathering as Nantor turned to face him. "You stupid wretch," he snapped. "Trying to distract me and then attack me! I'll show you how I repay such idiocy."

Helaine had finally understood why Score had been so cruel to her—it had served to amuse Nantor and catch him off-guard—and she now moved into action. Fighting was something she understood better than almost anyone else. "You can't hurt him—or me," she growled. "Because you need us to enable Eremin and Traxis to return. So I think we have the upper hand here." She let loose a fireball of her own, and this one worked properly. It flamed across the small room at Nantor.

His hand gestured, and a barrier sprang up. The fireball blazed out against it. "If you think I'll hold back because of that, you're even stupider than your boyfriend." He blasted a bolt back at her. Score barely had the time to use his chrysolite to call on his power of Water to douse the flames.

Helaine had dived to one side. "But we fight as a team," she pointed out. "And that makes a difference."

"Not a significant one." Nantor had all of Pixel's abilities, and that included the power of Fire. Score could feel him drawing on it, ready to launch another attack. Score beat him to it, drawing all of the water from the air in the room and from nearby, and hurled it at Nantor. At the same moment, Helaine used her chrysoprase, which gave her power over the element of Earth. This included anything taken from the earth, so she was able to rip sections of the metal floor and walls apart and throw them in his direction. Nantor didn't seem too worried, and he countered each of their moves.

But that didn't really matter, because what Nantor hadn't realized yet was that this was all a distraction, to keep him from seeing Score's real plan. When he had launched the fireball, his second spell had been to magically create smelling salts under the nose of the unconscious man on the floor. He was Section Supervisor Nine, the eyes and ears of the Overmind. Nantor had clearly blocked out the Overmind's mechanical devices in the room, preventing him from striking, but with the Supervisor awake again, the Overmind could see what was going on.

And act.

Score heard the sounds of people approaching down the corridor, and he grinned to himself—his plan had worked. Well, kind of . . . He had forgotten one small detail.

The Overmind didn't like him any more than it liked Nantor.

An armed squad burst in the door, each armed with the nasty, tube-like stun guns that Score had been subjected to before. He could remember the terrible pain that they induced, and as one of the new arrivals leveled a weapon at him, he knew he didn't want to feel it again.

Score had no option but to take the man out. He opened the floor under the man as he was preparing to fire. With a howl, the man fell through the hole into the basement. Score had to wonder if he'd done the right thing after all.

Two more of the squad opened fire on Nantor, who somehow managed to harden the air to prevent the blasts from reaching him. But it distracted him, and one of Score's blasts almost hit him.

"Give it up," Helaine called. "You can't fight all of us at once, and you know it. Surrender now while you still can."

"I do not surrender," Nantor growled, flinging fire at the recent arrivals. They threw themselves aside, but Nantor, unlike Pixel, had no qualms about injuring or killing anyone. One of the men caught a blast, and his clothes ignited. He began screaming horribly. Score was forced to use his own power over water to douse the flames, and then knock the man out by changing the air into knockout gas. The man would be in bad pain when he awoke, but hopefully he'd be able to get medical help.

The room had degenerated into utter chaos now. There were still half a dozen attackers firing their guns, mostly at Nantor, since he was clearly the biggest menace in the room. Dayta had scuttled across the floor to hide behind Score, clearly hoping he'd be able to protect her. Helaine was standing firm, flinging firebolts at Nantor. Score returned to the fight.

Despite his will, it was obvious that Nantor was now in trouble. He was being attacked on too many sides, and even with his skill with magic, he couldn't fight so many foes all at once. "Have to cut down the odds," he muttered. He set up a solid air shield that blocked the gun fire, and then sent a savage blast of fire directly at Helaine. She managed to block the flames by using magic to tear up some of the floor as a barrier, but she was starting to look really exhausted. Score wasn't in much better shape, especially with the magical distortion affecting his spells.

Nantor used the few seconds he had gained to start weaving a new spell. Score could feel the build-up of magical energy to a level that astonished him. It was far stronger than he could manage, and more than he'd have imagined possible of a Rim World. Nantor saw the look of surprise on his face, and laughed nastily.

"Don't think that your abilities are the highest point that can be reached," he sneered. "My power is far, far greater than yours, and I can do what you believe to be impossible. Witness!"

He gestured dramatically, and there was a sudden tearing in the air between Nantor and his attackers. It was a dark, gaping gash in space that Score knew well.

A portal.

"No," he muttered. "It's impossible. Nobody can create a portal *from* a Rim World."

Nantor laughed again. "Like I said, don't assume that because your powers are so limited that mine must be also. Despite what you believe, with sufficient power and control it *is* possible to construct a portal on a Rim World. And not only that . . ." He gestured again, and the magic flowed once more.

Score could feel power dragging at him. He stared in horror at the gash in space—the thing was starting to suck him toward it. Somehow Nantor had managed to make it suck at everyone in the room. Score felt himself being dragged across the floor toward the darkness.

Where did the portal lead? Obviously, not to anywhere good. Nantor was using it to remove some of his foes from this battle, and it was apparent which people he wanted gone—the portal was between Nantor and Score's party. The Overmind's security guards were on the far side of the room, by the door. They didn't seem to be affected by the power of the portal, though they all looked stunned and scared, clearly not knowing what the black gash in space was.

Dayta screamed. Score lunged for her as she was dragged past him, but his own footing was far from secure, and he couldn't quite reach her. She was drawn, arms and legs flailing helplessly, into the maw of the portal. She vanished from view, and her scream cut off abruptly. Wherever the portal led, Dayta was now there and no longer on Calomir.

Score fought against the pull of the portal, but it was a losing battle. Out of the corner of his eye, he could see that Helaine was doing better. She held fast onto the uprooted floorboards she'd been using as a shield, and seemed to be quite secure. But Jenna, like Score, had nothing to hold onto.

"I can't hold on," she gasped, reaching vainly toward Score. He tried to grab her hand, but couldn't manage it. He watched helplessly as she was sucked into the gash in space, and vanished, as Dayta had. Score fought against the drag, but he was losing ground. His only chance was that the power drain on Nantor—which had to be enormous to sustain the portal—would force him to shut it down before it drew Score in also.

But then he had second thoughts. Wherever the portal led, Dayta and Jenna were now there—and they had no way of getting back. Score respected Jenna's abilities, but the young girl's powers were almost all defensive and healing. If there was trouble on the far side of the gateway, Score was not at all sure Jenna could handle it. And Dayta would be even worse off—she was as naive as Pixel had once been. She'd grown up knowing nothing but virtual reality, and she'd be lost and helpless on an alien planet.

Could he leave them there, alone?

But could he go after them, and leave Helaine here to face Nantor without him? And, anyway, was there any guarantee that he could even do anything to help the two girls?

He was torn both ways. He wanted to stay here and help Helaine, but he was scared for Jenna and Dayta. He hesitated, and was lost. In a final surge of power, the portal dragged him in. As he entered it, he could feel that it was closing down behind him. Helaine was on her own now, left to face Nantor. Normally, Score would bet that Helaine could handle any foe—but Nantor was stronger, smarter, and nastier than she was, and Score knew she was in deep trouble.

Then again, he wasn't exactly rolling in comfort himself. He yelped as the portal spat him out at the far end, and then collapsed after him.

Score stared around him, Jenna and Dayta were already there, clutching one another for comfort amid their terror. Score couldn't blame them as he stared in shock at the last thing he had expected to see . . .

2

Helaine watched, stunned, as the portal closed behind Score, Jenna, and Dayta. It had been bad enough when Pixel—*no*! not really Pixel, *Nantor*—had somehow created a portal when it was supposed to be impossible. But now it was gone, and had taken with it all of her friends. She was left alone to face the deadly threat of Nantor.

Well, actually, not completely alone. The Overmind's guards were still present, and they were still a serious threat.

Nantor's shield holding back their fire was starting to crumble—he'd expended a lot of energy to make the portal and keep it open. He might be stronger and more skilled at magic use than Helaine, but out here on one of the Rim Worlds, there was only so much energy available to be used. And now Nantor was getting exhausted.

Helaine's main problem wasn't actually *fighting* Nantor—she was sure she could manage to stay alive and maybe even defeat him now that he was so weak—it was what to do once Nantor was beaten. She could hardly kill him without killing her friend, who apparently was still confined to some quarter of his own mind. Besides, though she enjoyed fighting, she didn't like to kill humans. The trouble was, if Nantor wasn't killed, then he could simply get his strength back and fight again. And, as far as she could see, there was no way to simply cast Nantor out of Pixel's body and restore her friend.

She wished that she was better at thinking things through, but the boys were the brains of the group for the most part. Pixel could piece together seemingly unsolvable mysteries, and even Score was pretty decent at working out plans. She didn't have the kind of subtle mind needed for such strategies. Given a problem, she liked to hack away at it, but that wasn't possible in this case.

Besides all of that, she was under a lot of pressure here. Despite the fact that magic was involved, the Overmind's guards didn't seem to be too thrown by the startling and unexpected events they had witnessed. No doubt because they were being controlled by the Overmind. The computer entity was new to the possibilities of magic, but it learned quickly. And though magic was powerful, it wasn't all-powerful— and on this world the Overmind *was* all-powerful. It controlled literally millions or even billions of people, and could call on any or all of them to push through its plans. And the Overmind was even smarter and sneakier than Pixel. It was a vast mind, somehow existing in that strange state of virtual reality that Pixel had once been a part of.

The fire from the guards was starting to make Nantor's shield crumble. More fighters had poured into the room, and were focused on the raging Nantor. He was getting exhausted from all the drains on his power, and this was making him furious and desperate.

"Still too many," he complained, launching another fire blast at the latest batch of guards. He glanced around the room, and Helaine could see that an idea had occurred to him. She didn't know what it was, but suspected that it wouldn't be very good for her, either. He suddenly threw a fireball behind him, at the wall that held the large video screen.

This exploded on impact, firing sharp, deadly shards of glass throughout the room. Helaine, warned by only seconds, had huddled down behind her barrier. She heard and felt the impact of the glass slamming into the flooring she'd raised up.

The guards, most of them quite exposed, didn't fare as well. She heard screams and then falling bodies, and didn't know if they were dead or just wounded. But Nantor laughed, and Helaine knew that he had won the immediate battle. But the Overmind wouldn't give up that simply, she was certain. There were many, many more fighters he could bring in against Nantor.

"Come on," the magician snarled, as he strode to where Helaine was hiding. "I need you for the next part of my plan."

"I will not go anywhere with you," Helaine said firmly, leaping to her feet. She wished she had a sword with her, even if she wouldn't be able to bring herself to turn it against the body of her friend. She simply felt better with the grip of one in her hand. She might be a magic user, but she was first and foremost a warrior, and she hated being in a battle without an edged weapon. "You cannot possibly win; surrender and restore Pixel."

"I can't understand why you want that wimp back!" Nantor howled. "He's so pathetic! Filled with soft, foolish emotions. You're a warrior, born to conquer and triumph. You are destined to be Eremin, Destroyer of Worlds. Stop fighting your destiny, and give in to your inner self."

"If Eremin is truly my destiny," Helaine said, softly, dangerously, "then I would sooner die here and now. I despise and loathe everything she believes in."

"Don't be stupid, girl," Nantor snapped. "She *is* you—the you that should be, the you that *must* be. You have the power, but she has the will and experience. Set her free. She is you as I am Pixel."

"You are *not* Pixel," Helaine replied with absolute conviction. "He has humanity and warmth, and cares for others. You care for only yourself and power."

"There *is* nothing else," Nantor answered. "But I don't have the time to stand here and discuss philosophy with you, girl. This Overmind creature has many minions it can call upon to fight its battles, and I've lost too much energy at the moment to successfully fight it. I have to retreat, and you must accompany me. I need you to bring Eremin back—and with her help, then I *know* I can defeat this creature."

"I will not come with you," Helaine repeated. She took a quick glance about the room, and saw that the guards were all down. Some were dead, most were badly wounded from the flying glass. There was blood everywhere, and it repelled even her, accustomed to warfare as she was. "You are sick and evil, and I will stop you." She reached out with her sapphire, intending to seize him and lift him off his feet. Instead, the magic twisted, and she ended up knocking him across the room.

"Idiot!" Nantor snarled. He readied a spell of his own, and then cocked his head, listening. "More guards," he complained. Frustrated and angry, he threw another fireball at her. Helaine flung herself aside. The blast narrowly missed her, and she could feel the heat singeing the tips of her long, dark hair. She batted out the flames, and looked around.

Nantor had disappeared, but more guards were pouring into the room. She started to get back to her feet when one of the men fired his tubular weapon at her.

There was an instant of terrible, searing pain, and then she mercifully lost consciousness.

When she struggled back to awareness, Helaine's entire body ached. At least the pain had gone, though the memory of it lingered. The events she had lived through flooded back to her, and she opened her eyes, wondering what fresh disaster she would be facing.

To her surprise, she was in a small room, lying on a bed. She moved slowly, trying not to aggravate her aches and pains, and managed to sit up. She was in some sort of a hospital room, and there was one other occupant. For a moment she didn't recognize the other girl, who was dozing in a chair. Then she remembered it was Pixel's old friend, Byte. Byte had been captured earlier by the Overmind, and had vanished.

"Byte," Helaine called. Her voice was weak, but it was enough to make the other girl jerk awake.

"Oh, Helaine!" Byte jumped to her feet. "Are you alright? You looked like you were dying when they brought you here."

"I am . . . in acceptable condition," Helaine lied. She was certain that this room was being monitored somehow by the Overmind, and she didn't want it to know how weak she felt. "How did you come to be here?"

"The Overmind was using me as a hostage, to try and get Pixel to do what it wanted," the blue-faced girl explained. "But something seems to have happened, and I wasn't needed as a hostage any longer, so I was brought here." She glanced around the room. Aside from the bed and her chair, it was completely empty. There was one door, but no sign of a handle or any way to open it.

"That's because Pixel is . . . gone." It was a lame explanation, but Helaine didn't know how to explain the terrible situation any better. "I hope he can be restored, but it is not likely as long as we are held prisoners. How long was I unconscious?"

"I'm not sure," Byte replied. "A couple of hours, at least. I've been kind of dozing myself."

Hours? Helaine winced. What had happened while she had been unconscious? Where were Score and Jenna? And what about Nantor? Byte clearly knew nothing, and what Helaine needed the most now was information.

"Overmind?" she called out, looking around the room. "I assume you're listening in."

"Of course," a pleasant, smooth voice answered. It seemed to come from everywhere in the room, and was neither male nor female. The far wall, blank until now, started to whirl with a kaleidoscope of color. "I find you strange humans quite intriguing."

"I'll bet," Helaine agreed, swinging to her feet. She felt light-headed, and had to sit still a moment. The after-effects of the pain blast, no doubt. "You've never seen anyone like us before."

"No," the Overmind agreed. "I find this . . . magic that you possess quite intriguing. It is something that I must acquire."

"It's not that simple," Helaine answered. "You have to be born with the ability—and you weren't born, were you?"

"No. But I do not feel the need to possess it personally—as long as my slaves have the ability, then I will be able to control it. That spacial incursion in the monitor room was most intriguing—how was it accomplished?"

Helaine didn't understand what he was talking about for a moment. She shook her head to try and clear it. "Oh, you mean the portal? I haven't a clue— I certainly couldn't manage anything like that. But Nantor has much more power than I have. Incidentally, did he get away?"

"For the moment," the Overmind replied. "But he cannot evade me for long."

"He can if he makes another portal," Helaine said. "Then he can just move to another world, and you won't be able to reach him."

"This is true—and it is one reason why I must discover how he manages that trick. I cannot allow someone as powerful as he is to challenge me and then escape. He must be brought under control again."

"Good luck," Helaine muttered. She wished she could concentrate more. Her brain felt like it was in a fog. That pain weapon left dreadful after-effects. It was odd, because the first time she was shot with one, she didn't have these problems.

Finally, it dawned on her. "What have you done to me?" she asked. "You've given me drugs or something, haven't you?"

"Naturally," the Overmind replied. "I did not believe you would cooperate with me otherwise. You have been given, among other things, a truth drug. It makes you answer my questions honestly. I told you, I must know all about this magic, and how to create it for my benefit. I spoke with the one you call Nantor when he was called Pixel. He made me understand that there are many worlds out there in the Diadem to which I can spread. I have reached the limits of my growth here on Calomir, and must send portions of myself to other worlds if I am to evolve."

Helaine felt sick, realizing that she was being forced to cooperate with this monster. But all she was forced to do was to tell the truth—and that meant she was still free to say what she felt. "You must *never* be allowed to leave this world," she gasped. "And you must be destroyed here, also. The people of this planet must be free to decide their own lives."

"For what?" the Overmind asked. "Before I existed, they were a contentious race—they fought one another, and killed one another. They engaged in dangerous activities. They allowed rampant emotion to guide their behavior. I stopped all of that. There is no war, no crime, no hatred. People do not risk their lives for foolish reasons. They are not ruled by chemical imbalances in their bodies, or foolish emotions. They live safely while young in virtual reality, where they may experience anything that they wish. And then they are protected when they mature."

"Protected?" Byte had been listening to the exchange so far without a word, but this was too much for her. "I have discovered the truth about the world you control," she growled. "You feed on our imaginations, and drain our will. The chips that you have inserted into our brains when we are born enables you to control our thoughts and actions. When we grow into adulthood, we become your slaves."

"It is for your own good," the Overmind argued. "I have brought peace to this planet, and a unity of thought."

"The peace of the graveyard," Byte yelled. "The unity of only your thoughts, your will! You have destroyed the minds of all adults to serve your corrupt and selfish pleasures."

"It is simply the way of evolution," the Overmind stated. "The weak fall, the strong rule. Your species must serve me, because I am the next stage in evolution. All is as it should be."

"No." Byte shook her head. "Helaine is right—you are evil, and corrupt, and you must be destroyed."

"You are acting emotionally," the Overmind said. "It is a human failing—one that you will be purged of in a few short years."

"I don't want to lose my emotions!" Byte yelled. "I don't want to lose my mind."

"It is inevitable."

Helaine had taken about as much of this dreadful computer mind as she could. "It is not," she broke in. "My friends and I will defeat you. We shall destroy you." She gave a weak laugh. "And that must be true—because I'm so full of your drugs that I can't possibly lie to you, can I?"

"I do not doubt that you believe it to be true," the Overmind agreed. "But that does not make it so. Your allies were sent through that space portal to some alien world, where they cannot help you. If they return, I shall have them dealt with. By then, I shall be able to manipulate magic myself."

"Don't be stupid," Helaine grumbled. She was starting to feel oddly tired. It was hard to remain sitting up. She wanted to lie down and go to sleep. "I told you, you'll never be able to do magic."

"No," agreed the monster. "But *you* can. And shortly you will be my slave, just as the rest of the humans on this world are."

"What are you talking about?" Helaine's voice was starting to slur, and she felt as if she was viewing the world from a far, far distance. "I don't have one of those stupid chips in my head. You can't control me."

"You don't have one *yet*," the Overmind said gently. "But there is a team of surgeons on their way to you now. The other drugs I gave you seem to be taking effect. You will be unconscious in a matter of minutes, and then they shall begin their work. When you awaken again, you will have a chip in your mind—and I will be able to take complete control of you. With you as my slave, I shall be able to understand and control magic, as I control everything else on this world."

"No," Helaine gasped. She tried to stay awake, tried to move, tried to do *anything*. But she found it impossible. The void was closing in on her, and there was nothing more she could do to fight it. But she had to! Otherwise she would lose her mind! She tried to fight the wave of unconsciousness, but it was impossible.

She fell back onto the bed, insensate.

3

Pixel was trapped inside of his own mind. It was terrifying, but he was forcing himself to stay calm, knowing that panic wouldn't help. When Nantor had used the chip in Pixel's brain to manifest himself again, the shock had sent Pixel into a kind of mental tumble. By the time he had recovered, Nantor was firmly in control of his body. Pixel discovered that he couldn't even manage to make a finger twitch.

He was still there, inside his mind, but unable to influence his body at all.

Nantor mostly seemed to disregard Pixel. He was certain that the younger mind would be either destroyed or absorbed in a short while, and Pixel knew that there was a real possibility of that happening. Nantor was far stronger than he was—he had had several hundred years to use his magic and grow. He could channel magic and use it in ways that staggered Pixel.

But there was one small thing that Nantor was overlooking in his arrogant dismissal of Pixel's abilities—the fact that they were still sharing a mind. Pixel couldn't exact *read* Nantor's mind—though they could talk to one another. Nantor generally ignored any attempts by Pixel to communicate, certain Pixel could say nothing that he wanted to hear. But Pixel could gain information when Nantor used his abilities. He now knew, for example, how to create a portal on a Rim World, something he had previously believed to be impossible. Not that the information would do him much good, because it took a delicacy of control over the flow of magic that he knew he simply didn't have. But it meant that he could gain access to other areas of Nantor's knowledge, and some of that might prove to be more helpful.

Right now, though, both Pixel and Nantor were facing the same problem. The Overmind had thrown in too many of his troops for even Nantor to take on alone. He had flung magic about like crazy, but there were always more fighters coming in. He'd been forced to flee the Administration Building, and had used his powers to seal the exits behind himself. The troops would be able to break out in a short while, but at least it gave Nantor time to catch his breath and to wonder what he could do next.

Pixel could "hear" him thinking. Nantor was furious and almost ready to spit blood. He wanted revenge on the Overmind, and then to get on with his work of freeing the other two members of the Three Who Rule. Helaine had been captured, so that meant going back into the building to free her so that Eremin could reclaim her body. But Nantor knew he couldn't manage the fight alone.

Pixel grinned mentally. "You're starting to see the advantages of cooperation," he told Nantor.

"Shut up," Nantor growled back. "You don't have much time left to you, and I don't intend to spend any of it talking to you. Just shut up and die."

"What, while I can help you?" Pixel chuckled soundlessly. "I know how you can get back into the building, and it's a way you'd never think of."

"And why should I believe anything *you* tell me?" Nantor asked. "You're weak, feeble, and soon to die. There's nothing that you can do that I can't, and you have absolutely no logical reason to help me."

"I have one," Pixel explained. "I want to get Helaine away from the Overmind, too. And if that means helping you to rescue her, then that's the way it has to be."

Nantor growled again. "I still can't trust you. And I don't need your help, anyway. You're pathetic."

"And you're still talking to me," Pixel replied. "Which shows that you don't have any better ideas, and aren't certain I'm so weak and useless. And, besides that, you were once me, so if I'm pathetic, what does that make you?"

"Powerful," Nantor answered. "I grew up. I understood what I could do. I achieved my true potential—which you never will."

"Potential?" Pixel was scornful. "Arrogance and selfishness aren't much of a potential. At least I use my abilities to help others."

"Helping others is foolish and unproductive. No matter how many you help, there are always more, mewling and crying out for your assistance, for you to squander your talents on their behalf. Scum, too pathetic to aid themselves, depending on you to help them. It's sickening to even think about doing it."

"You don't understand," Pixel sighed. "And you probably never will. With great power comes great responsibility."

"Ha!" Nantor snorted. "With great power comes great possibilities. You simply have to seize them—as I have done."

"Yeah, you did really well—you were beaten by Sarman, and then defeated again by Score, Helaine, and myself. Some potential!"

"But now I'm back again, and in control of this body that was once yours," Nantor pointed out. "And soon to be in sole possession of it. You are soon to be dead."

"But, in the meantime, you still need my help," Pixel said. "Because I can do things that you can't— like get back into the building."

"There's *nothing* you can do that I can't," Nantor snarled.

"There's one thing," Pixel contradicted him. "You see, I think very differently from you. You've forgotten how to do a lot that I can still achieve."

"Then prove it," Nantor said. "Tell me how I can get back into the building again."

"By cooperation," Pixel explained. "The one thing that would never occur to you. When Score, Helaine, and Jenna came to the Administration Building, it was with a group of rebels who are fighting the Overmind themselves. They're some of the people the Overmind can't directly control—their minds aren't affected by the chips, somehow. They want to free the ones who are enslaved, and they want to destroy the Overmind even more badly than you do. If you join forces with them, they will help you raid the building again."

Nantor was still unconvinced. "How can humans without even the slightest magical talents help me?"

"Because they understand *science*," Pixel replied. "They can fight the Overmind that way, a way you can't."

"How do you know all of this about them?" Nantor demanded. "You were a captive of the Overmind while your friends were with these fighters."

"The Overmind was monitoring them," Pixel answered. "I saw it all on the view screen."

Nantor considered his idea. Pixel could sense that he was reluctant to trust anyone else, and had a huge contempt for people who couldn't use magic. But, at the same time, the logic of what Pixel had been saying was starting to break through his arrogance. "I don't suppose it would hurt to talk to these people," Nantor finally conceded. "Where are they?"

"Not far," Pixel answered. "Take that side-street there—they're in a vehicle parked down the block."

"In a vehicle?" Nantor was moving in the indicated direction. "How many of them are there?"

"I'm not sure," Pixel admitted. "Four or five."

"Four or five?" Nantor stopped moving. "How can so few help *me*? The Overmind has an army."

"Those four or five are highly motivated and can think for themselves," Pixel argued. "The Overmind's minions are just obeying its explicit orders. All we need to do is to disrupt those orders, and they'll be next to useless to it. And, besides, there's another potential source of soldiers for us—all of the Drones."

"The Drones?"

"They're the workers whose minds have been drained almost entirely by the Overmind," Pixel explained. "They need a lot more control, but once they're started, they would be almost unstoppable. If we can override the Overmind's control of them, and use them on *our* side, then we can't lose."

"There are far too many *ifs* in that idea to suit me," Nantor grumbled.

"Well, I don't hear you coming up with any better ideas," Pixel pointed out. Something had occurred to him. "Hey, if you're me, sort of, does that mean that you came from this world originally, too?"

"Yes," Nantor answered, slowly.

"Then how come you don't know anything about computers?"

"Because I'm a lot older than you, you moron," Nantor said. "I was born long before there were any such things on Calomir. I left this world to enter the circuit of the Diadem before there was anything resembling the Overmind."

"Ah." Pixel's curiosity was satisfied. "So you knew your parents, then?"

"Of course I did—very dull, dreary, and stupid people."

"It seems I never knew my own parents," Pixel said, wistfully. He was sure Nantor's parents weren't as bad as the magician claimed.

"You missed nothing," Nantor growled.

"I missed *everything*," Pixel replied. "I'm only just starting to understand how much I lost out on. Score's mother died when he was young, and his father is a crook. Helaine's mother died, too, and her father is . . . well, difficult at best. And my parents—I don't even know who they were. It seems as if we all had family troubles. I really envy people with normal lives."

"Normal lives are dull and boring," Nantor snapped. "*We* have power, and need nobody. Friends, families, and lovers are all pointless—power is all that counts."

"I feel sorry for you," Pixel said, and was surprised to discover that he really did. "I have this ache inside me from not knowing my parents. But I have a wonderful warmth from having friends like Score and Helaine, and even more from having a person like Jenna who loves me. *That's* what makes my life worth living—not some stupid pursuit of power over other people. Even you might become a halfway decent person if you *cared* about somebody other than yourself."

"The arrogance of youth," Nantor sneered. "You think you know better than me? I have several hundred years worth of experiences and wisdom over you. Love? Ha! Love doesn't last, and neither do people—especially ones without the power to extend their own lives. They're *nothing*, except for what use they can be to me. Emotional attachments are part of the foolishness of childhood—adults grow out of them."

"I will never outgrow them!" Pixel vowed.

"That's true enough," Nantor jeered. "Because your life-span is severely limited. You won't last more than a few days."

"You won't get rid of me that easily," vowed Pixel, even though he didn't have a clue how to make that boast come true. "But even if you did, my life will have been infinitely more worthwhile than yours."

"Moron!" Nantor cried. "I have the power to rule worlds, to shape destinies, to destroy planets. I shape, control, and rule. And you just bleat about love."

"You have the power to harm," Pixel agreed. "But you also have, if you wished to use it, the power to help and to heal."

"Why should I do such things?" asked Nantor. "They're a waste of my time and energies."

"Well, right now they aren't," Pixel pointed out. "Because by cooperating with the rebels here, you will be able to take on the Overmind again—and have a better chance of winning."

"I'm still to be convinced of that," Nantor grumbled. "But I have agreed to try. And if it fails, they will not have to worry about the Overmind ever again. I personally will slaughter the entire lot of them. So bear *that* in mind when you make your plans. And if I detect even the slightest hint that you're playing me for a fool, or are plotting to retake your body, then I will also kill them. Their lives . . ." Nantor laughed. "I almost said *are in your hands*, but that's not true, is it? You don't *have* any hands any longer. And soon you will have nothing at all . . ."

Pixel wished he could sigh, or scream, or do anything. But he was still locked in this small corner of his own mind. And everything hinged on his being able to convince and control an unstable, arrogant, and power-crazed maniac to behave himself . . .

What chance did he have of succeeding?

4

Jenna stared all around in astonishment where she had landed. She'd been through portals before, and was used to some strange worlds, but this one was by far the oddest she had ever seen. Even Pixel's planet seemed normal compared to this! Beside her, Dayta seemed just as confused. Jenna looked over at Score, who had an bewildered look on his face.

"Do you know where we are?" she asked him.

"Oh, yes," Score answered, grinning. "I do indeed know where we are—home."

Jenna stared at the tall buildings, the speeding, noisy, smelly vehicles, and the aloof, hurrying people who were dressed very oddly. "This is not *my* home."

"But it *is* mine," Score said. "This is New York. Welcome to the Big Apple, girls."

The three of them were sitting on hard stonelike material in the mouth of an alley. Garbage was piled up in black plastic bags, and in metal and plastic cans. The stench was appalling. "Perhaps we could move from here?" Jenna suggested.

"Yeah, good thinking." Score bounced to his feet and helped both of the girls up. Then he gave Dayta a critical stare. "You're going to be kind of hard to explain. I mean, I think you look just great, but blue skin and pointy ears aren't really the accepted norm around here. You may get some stares, even some comments."

Dayta touched her face. "Is there some stigma on this world to do with blue skin and unusual ears?" she asked, worried.

"Well, let's just say that it's not normal, and that might get you noticed. Don't let people bug you."

"They give one another insects on your world?" Jenna asked. "It seems like an odd medium of exchange."

"No, they use good old-fashioned money," Score replied. He reached into one of the pockets of his jeans and pulled out some leaves of paper. "I always carry a few dollars around with me, just in case." His face lit up. "Hey, let's find a pizza parlor—I could really go for a good slice or two of New York's finest."

Jenna gripped his arm. "Obviously you are anticipating enjoying eating, but we have more important things to do. We must get back to Calomir and help Pixel and Helaine."

"Sweetie," Score answered, "I'm as worried about them as you are. But, right now, there's nothing we can do about it. Neither of us has the power or skill to create a portal on a Rim World. And Dayta there has zero magic." His eyebrows raised. "Speaking of which, it's a good job that Pixel—er, Nantor—didn't send us to some world deeper in the Diadem. Without any magic, she'd not stand much of a chance of survival."

Dayta snorted. "I'm tougher than you think. Besides, if I understand this magic business right, the deeper into the Diadem you go, the more power you have, right?" When Score nodded, she smiled. "Then Nantor would have been stupid to send you to a world where you'd get more power, and could conjure up a portal that would take you back again to face him. It's much more logical to send you to a world you can't escape from, and where you have no greater powers, isn't it?"

Score laughed, and looked at Jenna. "I wonder if they're all this logical and bright on Calomir? I do believe she's figured that out." He patted Dayta's shoulder. "Smart thinking. Anyhow, we can't get off the Earth unaided, and we need to discuss where we go and what we do. Now, we could do it standing here on a busy, noisy street, or we could do it while we eat and drink and sit down. Which is it?"

Jenna's stomach was reminding her that it had been a while since she ate. "I guess we go hunting for this odd food of yours," she agreed. "Is it difficult to find?"

"Not in New York," Score replied, with a grin. "Stick close to me, or we'll get separated, and that could make things difficult. It's a big city, and there are lots of people."

"I'm not at all sure I like it," Dayta said. "There are so many people, it's not natural."

"That's because you're used to virtual reality," Score said. "Real reality is a bit messier—and smellier." He took her hand in his left, and Jenna's in his right.

"Okay, stick with me, girls." He started off, and they had no option but to follow.

Jenna used the opportunity to examine this world and its peoples. Score was correct in saying that there were no other blue-skinned folk about. Indeed, light and dark seemed to be the main colors here, though there was a lot of variety in the levels of each color. And while most of the males seemed to wear similar clothing—trousers and shirts, though of differing styles and colors—the women wore all kinds of strange things. Many were dressed in similar fashion to the men, but others wore dresses or skirts. What astonished—and, truthfully, embarrassed—Jenna the most was the amount of skin that they were willing to expose to even casual bypassers. Some had skirts that showed almost all of their legs. Others wore tops that showed a great deal of cleavage. It was very immoral, as Helaine had warned her. Helaine had been to this world before, and had been just as shocked by local customs. What surprised her, though, was that most of the men seemed to ignore the immodest women. Some would glance at the sights, but most seemed to be uninterested. Perhaps it was a case of simply having too much available to look at. She was glad that she wore a modest, full-length skirt, though, and not clothing like the locals. Although, if Pixel were around it might be fun . . .

Pixel! She'd been avoiding thinking about him. But his memory was a sharp pain in her heart. She didn't know what had happened to him, but his body was clearly possessed by this Nantor character. Was it a permanent possession, or could she help to restore the Pixel she loved? She didn't know, and it hurt her badly. She felt as if she'd run off and left him, even though there had been no choice for her in the matter. She wanted to ask Score what he thought—but she was afraid of what he might answer. Besides, she knew that—however much of a cheerful front he put up—he had to be worried sick about Helaine. The two of them had never made any public display of affection—quite the opposite in fact, they usually fought—but Jenna could tell they felt very deeply for one another. Leaving Helaine alone to face Nantor must be eating at Score.

He certainly seemed to cover it up well, though. He led the two girls into a small building. Despite her worries and stresses, Jenna couldn't help enjoying the delightful smells in the place. There were small tables made of some sort of shiny material, and a few people were sitting at them eating or sipping drinks. One of the young men looked up and grinned as he saw Dayta.

"Whoa!" he called out. "Cool costume! Live long and prosper."

It was evidently some sort of localized greeting, and Dayta promptly smiled and repeated it back to him, which made the youngster grin even more. He muttered something about *Star Trek fans*—whatever they were—and went back to eating.

Score, meanwhile, had ordered the three of them slices of what he referred to as "pepperoni pizza" and sodas. Jenna had tasted soda before, since Score enjoyed transforming water into soda for most of his meals, but he'd never tried making pizza with his powers. He always claimed he could never get it right.

They sat together at a table, and Jenna took a nervous bite. Some of Score's ideas about what things were good were often not hers—like his fondness for bare legs in girls. But she discovered that he was quite correct about this pizza. "It's delicious," she exclaimed, and took another bite. Dayta, having watched Jenna try it first, did the same.

"Didn't I tell you?" Score asked, looking proud of himself. "New York pizza can't be beat."

"And speaking of *can't be beat*," Dayta said. "What are we going to do now? How do we get back to

Calomir, and how do we stop Nantor—and the Over-mind?"

Score shook his head. "That's not the main question right now," he said. Jenna couldn't believe what he'd said.

"You're going to just abandon Pixel?" she gasped.

"I didn't say that, and I wouldn't do that," Score replied firmly. "But you two girls aren't yet seeing the big picture. The normal flow of magic has been altered. Spells are starting to go all wonky. And there's only one thing that can cause that—there's serious trouble on Jewel."

"What's Jewel?" Dayta asked. "And why should I care about this flow of magic? It's nothing to me—I can't do it anyway."

"Jewel is the world at the center of the Diadem," Score explained. "It seems to be the source of all magic. The further from it you get, the weaker the power of magic. We're still on the Rim here on Earth, so it's quite weak compared to the strength on Jewel. But magic is unstable, and needs to be controlled. On Jewel there's something called the Diadem Analog—a representation of all the worlds of the Diadem made from gemstones. And each gem is imbued with the spirit of the world it represents. Nantor's essence was powering the jewel for Calomir after we trapped him in it. Now he's broken free somehow, and that jewel is empty. And that's throwing off the balance of magic. Until the balance is restored, the spells that any magician casts could go wrong—maybe even horribly, fatally wrong. And magic is our only real weapon against both Nantor and the Overmind. If we were to go back to Calomir while the magic is wonky, it would be dangerous, and maybe even fatal." He looked at the two girls, and Jenna could see the pain in his eyes that he'd been trying to cover up with his habitual humor. "You *must* know I want to go back to save Helaine and Pixel. But while magic is going crazy, that's a stupid option. What we need to do, first and foremost, is to see if we can somehow balance out the Analog again."

"You're saying we have to go to Jewel, not Calomir," Jenna said slowly. "And only then can we help our friends."

"Yes." Score sighed. "I hate leaving Helaine and Pixel to fend for themselves. And I hate leaving your planet in the control of that mutant monster Overmind," he added to Dayta. "But we *have* to get magic working right again. Can you see that?"

Jenna nodded slowly. "Yes, it does make sense. But my heart isn't interested in sense—I just want Pixel safe."

"I promise," Score said, gripping her wrist. "I *promise* that we'll not abandon him. But we have to do this first." He looked at Dayta. "Do you understand?"

"Not really," she confessed. "I mean, this magic stuff is totally alien to me. I deal in science and logic. But what you're saying does seem to make sense. Science and logic created the Overmind, and it's using them to maintain its power over my people. Magic would seem to be the only power we have over it, so getting your magic working again is a priority."

"Wait a moment. "Jenna scowled at Score. "How can Dayta come with us? Won't the increased magic in the Inner Worlds kill her?"

"Nope," Score answered, with something like one of his old grins. "It only affects magic-users. Humans live on the other planets, and as long as they have no magical ability, the increased power can't affect her. Kind of like squirrels running along power lines—as long as they're not in touch with the ground, the power can't hurt them. Dayta's our very own squirrel."

"Okay, so traveling there wouldn't kill her," Jenna agreed. "But you're forgetting one major problem—

we're on Earth, and that means we don't have the power or skill to open a portal to another world. And Shanara can't help because she doesn't know we're here—she's expecting us to be on Calomir. We can't contact her from here."

Score grinned again. "Ah, but we *can* contact Oracle. One of the earliest spells I ever learned was a summoning spell for him. If you recite it with me, we can bring him here, and then he can go back to Shanara and have her create a portal for us."

Jenna managed a smile herself. "You know, you're not as stupid as you act sometimes."

"Thanks," Score said. "I think. Okay, eat up. We need to find somewhere quiet to do this. Maybe New York is taking pretty blue-skinned girls in its stride, but even the most laid-back New Yorker is likely to find people appearing from nowhere to be a bit odd."

Jenna wolfed down the last of her delicious pizza, and washed it down with the remains of her soda. Dayta and Score did the same, and then they left the store and slipped into a quiet back street.

"This should do it," Score decided. "Right, Jenna, just focus on helping me." he muttered a spell under his breath, and she worked to reinforce it. But she felt the magic *twist* and go wrong. Instead of their black-clad friend appearing, a small boat made of leather popped into existence. "Not much help," Score sighed. "That's a *coracle* . . ." He gestured, and it vanished back to wherever it had come from. "We'd better try again, while we still have the power." He muttered the spell again, and Jenna backed him up.

This time she felt that the magic was working properly. A moment later, Oracle himself appeared. He looked rather startled, as did Dayta when she saw the black-clothed man appear from nowhere.

"This world is hardly Calomir.

Something's amiss, I rather fear."

Jenna frowned. "What's with the bad rhyming?" she asked.

"I wish it was just that he wants to become a rap star," Score answered. "But it's what happens to him when magic goes crazy—he has to speak in verse. It's so irritating that I'm more motivated to solve the problem of magic just to shut him up than to save the universe." He turned to Oracle. "Okay, as little of that annoying talking as possible. Somehow Nantor is back, and he's taken possession of Pixel's body. Worse, this has thrown magic out of order again. So we need to get to Jewel and check on things there. You have to get Shanara to create a portal to get us back to her, so we can go deeper into the Diadem and solve the problem. Then we have to get back and save Pixel and Helaine. Oh, yes, and Calomir as well. Right, let's get busy."

Oracle looked at him and then shook his head.

"What you ask I cannot do.

"If Nantor's back, then so might you."

Jenna was confused. "What's he talking about? He's making no sense. Why won't he help us?"

Score bit at his lower lip. "Actually, he *is* making sense, of a sort. He's afraid that if Nantor is back, then maybe Traxis has taken control over me, too, and this is just a trick." He turned to Oracle. "Look, if I were Traxis, I wouldn't be asking for help—I'd be issuing orders, wouldn't I?"

"On Earth you're trapped unless I aid.

I will not be by you betrayed."

"*That* I understand," Jenna said, annoyed at their friend. She glared at him. "Score's fine, and still himself. Traxis couldn't be faking that. So you *will* do as he asks, and get Shanara to set up the portal." She was gripping her citrine as she said this, and using the full force of persuasion that she possessed. Oracle could not refuse her.

"As you command, then I obey,

"And soon you shall be on your way."

He promptly vanished. Jenna almost collapsed from relief.

"Okay," Score said. "As soon as we get to Shanara's castle, we explain the problem to her, and get her to send us deeper into the Diadem. We've got to do this as fast as possible, while there's still a chance of helping out on Calomir." he looked concerned. "I know Helaine can hold out until then," he added softly. Jenna knew he was in real pain over leaving her.

A black gash in the air formed just in front of them, and Jenna's spirits rose. The way off Earth! "Let's go," she said, decisively. She gripped Dayta's hand, and stepped through the portal. Score was right behind her.

The two girls emerged inside Shanara's castle. Watching them anxiously was Shanara herself, with Blink on a nearby table. Oracle, too, was watching. The portal closed behind them.

And something was very wrong.

There was no sign of Score.

Jenna was completely bewildered. "What happened?" she asked. "Score was right with us—but he's not here. Where is he?"

Shanara turned pain-filled eyes toward her. "Gone," she said, softly. "He's dead."

5

Score found himself confused and astonished for the second time after stepping through a new portal. Only this time it wasn't a pleasant surprise, as New York had been. He was standing alone in the middle of what looked like some wild, alien jungle. There were trees of strange sorts, bushes, and other plants.

"What the heck?" he muttered, trying to turn back to the portal. It had already closed behind him, though, leaving him here alone. Where were the two girls he had been following? And why wasn't he in Shanara's castle, as he was supposed to be?

The magic must have gone wrong again, somehow. But . . . if it *had*, then why weren't Jenna and Dayta here with him? Surely the portal couldn't have shifted *after* it had been formed?

At least . . . not accidentally, at any rate.

Score thought back, concentrating on his feelings. Whenever magic went wrong, he could feel it as a sort of twisting in his stomach. There had been no such feeling when he'd stepped through the portal—so the magic had gone right.

Except . . . obviously it hadn't, because he was alone and lost on some alien planet he'd never seen before. How could this have happened? He tried to figure out some way that things might have gone wrong, stranding him here, but he couldn't imagine any. There was only one possible answer . . . that this had been a deliberate trap.

And that meant something he *really* didn't want to believe. That he'd been betrayed by Oracle and Shanara. They had been the ones to set up the portal, and if nothing had gone wrong with it, then it must have done what they had wished. So they had *planned* on sending him here.

Why? He couldn't figure it out. If there was some sort of a problem they needed him to deal with, they would have surely told him about it first. Or, if it had cropped up at the very last second, somehow, Oracle would have come to meet him and explain things. But Oracle wasn't here, even though Oracle had to know where *here* was . . .

It didn't look very pleasant at all. Why would Oracle and Shanara dump him here on this planet? It didn't make any sense to Score at all. They were his friends, and they had helped him any number of times in the past. Why would they suddenly do something like this to him? And without explanation? He simply couldn't understand it. This was not like them.

Still, getting answers wouldn't be too difficult. He could tell by the flow of magic about him that he'd shifted from a Rim World to the next level, and he had more magical power to draw upon. He wouldn't need Jenna's help this time to use his powers to summon Oracle. And when that traitor appeared, Score would get some answers! He wasn't sure how he could force the image to speak—since he wasn't actually real in the way normal people were. He couldn't exactly be threatened, and Score didn't possess Jenna's power to compel people. But he was sure he'd think of something.

He didn't get a chance. He felt more than saw something heading toward him at great speed, and he barely threw himself aside in time. A long, woody tendril flickered through the place he'd just been standing, and then snapped back like a whip. Score rolled on the ground and came back to his feet facing a large tree. But it was like no tree he had ever seen before.

It was about thirty feet tall, and looked normal—if you could somehow ignore the long, thin branches that were whipping about in the air. There was very little breeze, and it certainly wasn't the wind that made those tendrils move. As Score stared at the tree in shock, another one of the branches lashed out at him. He dived aside again, and the branch snapped back again.

The tree could somehow sense him! And it had lightening-fast reactions. Already another branch was moving. Score didn't have any time to think things through—he simply conjured up a ball of fire and threw it at the tree. The wood caught fire, and the branches lashed and thrashed about even more as the flames ate at the tree.

Score stared at the tree in astonishment. Trees were things that didn't move much at all—not things that could lash out like this one had been doing! This was some alien planet all right! Score started to turn away, and then had to dive quickly to one side.

A strange *something* whooshed through the spot where Score had been standing. He barely caught a glimpse of what looked like some mutant form of tumbleweed before the thing somehow braked, spun and shot back toward him. This one had tendrils, too, but instead of lashing out, they had large, sharp thorns on them. This mobile plant was trying to run him down like a car! And then stab him to death with the thorns!

Score moved aside as the bizarre plant shot at him a second time. The thorns were trying to slash him, but he managed to stay out of their reach. The plant halted, and started to move toward him again.

It didn't get a chance. Another of the lashing tendrils snapped out, and wrapped around the plant. It was lifted from its . . . well, obviously *feet* wasn't the word, but neither was *roots* . . . Flailing about, it was hauled toward another of the tall trees. The tendril dropped the thorn-plant into an opening in the top of the trunk. Score heard a crunching sound, and then the tendrils started trying to reach him, too.

He started to move off, watching over his shoulder as he did so. What kind of an insane planet was this? Plants and trees that could move and hunt? Weird, squared! He wondered if they were the only oddities here, or whether the entire world was insane. He kept a careful watch as he walked briskly away from the hunting trees. He could see movement among the trees, and then the tendrils would lash. Sometimes they would seize things, but most of the time they missed. It looked like the forest he was in was composed mainly of these hunter-trees. Even the bushes were quivering, and he didn't think it was from either the wind or excitement.

Keeping out of range of the tendrils wasn't easy, but he was helped slightly by the fact that the hunting trees couldn't grow too close to one another. If they did, they would attack each other until one was torn apart—generally the younger one. The rolling balls of thorns took advantage of the safe paths between the hunters. They were not rooted, and somehow they could roll along at about twenty miles an hour. Score didn't know how they did it, but they could somehow sense prey, even though they had no eyes or any other sensory organ that he could detect.

And every single tree and plant here seemed to be interested in eating him.

He didn't see any other animal life at all, not even birds. Well, that kind of figured. On most planets, birds nested in trees. Here, that would be instantly fatal. And lots of animals used trees for nests, or feeding— and here the trees did the feeding. Animal life—except for him—didn't seem to exist at all. This was a world where the plants had evolved into strange and lethal varieties. "Slay it with flowers," he muttered. Here a corsage could kill you!

Which led him to another nasty thought. Oracle and Shanara had clearly left him here on purpose. Which meant that they could hardly be unaware of the murderous nature of the plant-life here. Which meant that they were trying to kill him.

But why? He simply couldn't understand it. He had been certain that they were his friends, so to betray him like this was completely unlike them. And yet they clearly were after his death. Maybe they had been taken over by some magical means, and forced to do this? Oracle *had* been acting oddly when they had summoned him to Calomir. Was it possible that the Overmind had somehow taken over Oracle and Shanara?

No, that couldn't be the right answer. The Over-mind needed a computer chip in the brain to be able to command anyone, and Oracle didn't have a tangible brain. And Shanara hadn't gone anywhere near Calomir . . .

Some other wizard, then? There had been that one who'd caused all of the trouble on the planet Brine, for example. They never had figured out who he or she was, or where. It might be possible that a wizard had cast a spell, but there was no way to discover if that was what had happened while he was stranded here.

What Score needed to do was to summon Oracle again and try to get some answers and help. But he'd need to be able to concentrate to do that. And to con-centrate, he'd need some peace and quiet.

Which he certainly wasn't going to get around here. As he walked briskly, tendrils from the trees lashed fu-tilely at him. Rolling thorn balls attacked him, and he was forced to defend himself. Sometimes he flamed them, but mostly he just tricked them into getting too close to the hunting trees, which snatched them up and chomped on them.

Then a new problem turned up—quite literally. He was walking warily along when he suddenly spotted what looked like old ropes on the ground ahead. Deciding that caution was certainly called for here, he felt sure that even old ropes spelled trouble on this planet. Using his power of transformation, he shaped some of the air above the rope into the image and weight of a squirrel, and let it drop onto the ground.

The "ropes" immediately whipped out, circling the "squirrel" before it could move. Then, to his astonishment, there was the crackle of ozone, and the stench of frying. His "squirrel" vanished into nothingness again, and the "ropes" went back to playing dead.

"An electrical plant," Score muttered to himself. If he got too close to *that*, he'd be grabbed and shish-kabobed in seconds! So there was another peril to watch out for. He detoured around the trap, and kept on moving.

This was certainly not a planet for vegetarians! Here the salads would eat *you*! It was a strange and terrible world, and he couldn't relax for a second. There seemed to always be something new, lurking, looking for food.

Some of the plants were relatively normal, and stayed fixed in one spot. Others, like those rolling thorn balls, moved about, looking for prey. There were no flowers, Score noticed, and then realized why—flowers attracted insects and birds to pollinate them.

On *this* planet, any insects or birds wouldn't be pollinating—they'd be eaten. So there was no need for flowers. Score found himself wishing for just a splash of color to relieve the unending shades of green.

Green . . . Biology hadn't been one of his best subjects at school—well, actually, skipping school had been what he was best at—but he did remember something. Plants were green because they contained chlorophyll. And that made food for the plant from sunlight. So the plants here still made their own food . . . Yet they also ate anything that came within reach. Then he understood why—because chlorophyll made energy slowly. And these plants all seemed to move pretty fast—so they needed a quicker source of energy, which generally meant eating other living things.

It sounded like a circular sort of reasoning—the plants here were fast because they needed to catch food—and the food they caught enabled them to move fast. It was a hellish world. And one he'd been deliberately sent to by people he'd always believed were his friends.

It seemed quite clear that Shanara and Oracle were trying to kill him. And, judging by the fact that he was getting very tired, and his magic was getting depleted, their aim might succeed. He could fight off the attacks if he was alert, but he simply couldn't keep it up forever. It was far too exhausting. And he couldn't stop fighting and concentrate on getting off this world because there was never any let-up in the attacks.

As traps went, he had to admit, this was a beauty.

If Helaine, or Pixel, or even Jenna were here, it wouldn't be so bad. They could take turns fighting and resting. But alone . . . he didn't stand a chance. As soon as his energies ran down, he'd be plant food. Judging from the exhaustion that had settled upon him, it wouldn't take a very long time, either. He was getting near the end of his reserves.

Thinking of the others made him realize just how much he missed them. He'd grown up—well, oddly. His father was a minor New York gangster, who had spent most of his time and efforts in getting money by whatever illegal methods might work. He could barely recall his mother, except that she'd been very pretty, and always frightened. She'd died when he was young, and her face was kind of hazy in his memory. He'd been nine . . . no, he realized suddenly, that wasn't right! It couldn't be! He was only thirteen—almost fourteen—now, so if she'd died only four years ago, he should have a lot more memories of her.

And he also knew in his mind that she'd died when he was six.

This didn't make any sense. She couldn't have died twice.

Could she?

He'd discovered on Helaine's home world a tapestry of a long-lost queen. And the image had looked exactly like Score's memories of his mother. Was it possible that she had been from Ordin? When Score had first become involved in the Diadem, he'd found a paper left by his mother that had clues in it about his future. How could she possibly have known about that? Score's father had explained that his mother had been a *strega*—a wise woman, or a witch, "from the old country." Score had always assumed that "the old country" was Italy, but maybe it wasn't.

He was thinking so hard that he almost died. At the very last second, he realized that something was hurtling swiftly toward his head. He threw himself aside, and a large, heavy thorn narrowly missed him.

Another killer plant! He looked around and spotted this new one. It was a large shrub, maybe six feet tall, and it had odd vines with many of these thorns attached. As he watched, one of the vines suddenly snapped like a bow string, and another thorn was launched directly toward him.

He ran, thorns whistling in the air about him. This was getting *really* tiring now! But he couldn't stop for a breather, because it might be his last such break. Was he doomed to go on until he collapsed, exhausted, too weak to fight off the killer vegetation? If only Helaine were here! He missed his other friends, but he discovered that he was missing her far more. She was still on Calomir, perhaps in deadly trouble herself. Did she think he'd run out on her? Was she contemptuous of him? Or was she as afraid for him as he was for her?

He realized that he was getting awfully fond of the female warrior. At least thinking about her seemed to give him more energy. "She's totally the wrong person for me," he told himself. "She's everything I'm not— noble, proud, brave, arrogant, strong, annoying . . ." But none of that really mattered, he knew. He trusted her, as he'd never trusted another human being since his mother had died. He knew he could rely on Helaine to help him no matter what dangers they faced. And, even more strangely, he knew he'd risk his own life to help her when she was in trouble. He'd never felt that way about anyone before.

Having friends was dangerous to your health!

But he *had* to survive! Not only for his own sake, but also because Helaine would be depending upon him for help. If she were okay, she'd have found some way by now to be *here*, helping him. She often said she wasn't the world's best thinker and planner, but she always found a way. She was a lot smarter than she gave herself credit for. So, since she wasn't here, it meant that she still needed his help.

His help! He was barely alive now, battered and exhausted, and any second might make the mistake that would kill him. He couldn't help himself, so how could he ever imagine he could help her? But he knew that he simply couldn't abandon her. There had to be some way out of this—there *had* to be!

And then he spotted—well, not the way out, but at least a way to rest a while. The landscape had changed slightly, and he was now in a series of low hills and valleys. And, even better, he saw a dark shadow on one valley wall that could only be a cave. These plants needed sunlight to produce energy, so they couldn't possibly live inside a dark cave! He made his way there, using the last dregs of his magical power to destroy any plants in his way. He dragged himself into the cave opening, and looked around.

As he'd been praying, the cave was devoid of life. He would be safe in here for a while. Then the sun would go down, and this planet would sleep for a while. The vegetation couldn't get him in here, so he could rest.

Then he'd summon Oracle, and—

And what? He couldn't force Oracle to help him; Jenna was the one with the ability to persuade people to do things. And Oracle wasn't quite real, so none of Score's magic abilities would be any good against the image of the man. And if he couldn't *force* Oracle to help him, it was very unlikely that Oracle would help him of his own free will. This must have been a trap laid at least with his help, so he was hardly likely to want to free Score.

So, what could he do? He needed a portal off this planet, and before morning. Actually, a lot sooner than that, if he could. He had people to help and another world to save.

If only he wasn't stuck here in this cave!

6

When Helaine awoke, she felt groggy and unfocused. She tried to sit up, but the effort was too much for her, and she collapsed back, weakly.

There was movement in the room, and then she heard a girl's voice. "Here, drink some of this. It should help you." Something was pressed to her lips, and Helaine was forced to swallow the liquid she was offered or choke. It was cool, but somehow warmed her throat as she drank. She could feel a little strength returning to her body, and her mind started to uncloud.

She opened her eyes, and found she was looking up at Pixel's friend, Byte. The girl's face was drawn with worry and tiredness, but she was trying to force a friendly smile. "How are you feeling?"

"Terrible," Helaine admitted. "But not as terrible as I was a couple of minutes ago." She struggled, and managed to sit up in the bed, and examine her surroundings. She was in a small room, probably some sort of a hospital. She was in a loose gown instead of her street clothes. She reached up to her head. The Overmind had said that his surgeons would be implanting a chip there. But she could feel no bandage, no wound, and not even a sore spot. "Didn't they do the operation?"

"Oh yes," Byte said, grimly. "You've been unconscious since they brought you back three hours ago."

Helaine couldn't understand it. She felt her head again. "But there's no scar, or anything. And I can't *feel* the chip."

"They're really good at this implanting business," Byte said bitterly. "It's a very quick job, under five minutes, and the wound is healed up artificially. And you won't feel the chip until the Overmind activates

78

it—and then you'll feel nothing else. I talked to some of the medical staff—one of them gave me that drink for you—and they told me all about the chips. The doctors can't be controlled by the Overmind because they wouldn't be able to operate if they were, so they're free. Except they all have chips of their own, and if they ever refuse an order, the Overmind wipes their brains out. They're forced to perform the operations or become mindless slaves."

"So they elect instead to turn other people into slaves," Helaine said, bitterly.

"Don't judge them too harshly," Byte requested. "What else can they do?"

"They can *fight*," Helaine growled. "And they can die rather than force other people to become slaves." Anger was helping her strength to return. "Cowards can always find ways to justify their actions—or inactions. It doesn't make them right." She swung her feet out of the bed. "Do you know where my clothes are?"

Byte glanced around the windowless room. "There's a small closet behind that door," she answered. "Maybe they're in there."

"Take a look," Helaine ordered. "If I am to fight, it will be easier if I'm dressed in something other than this hospital gown."

"You can't fight!" Byte protested. "You're still too weak from the operation. You have to rest. The doctors ordered it."

"Another excuse for cowardice," Helaine scoffed. "I *can* fight because I *must* fight. I will not surrender to this Overmind, and it will be forced to attempt to control my mind. It is possible that I shall lose that fight, so I must do what I can before it attempts to control me. If it thinks I am too weak to fight, then *now* is the time to act."

"And what do you think you can do?" Byte asked. "Can't you see that this is hopeless? The Overmind is stronger than you or me. We can't possibly defeat it."

"More excuses bred in cowardice," Helaine growled. "If you think you can't beat it, then you certainly *can't* beat it. You have already lost the battle. How can you be so cowardly when Pixel is so brave? Don't you have any of your friend's strength?"

"I'm not a coward!" Byte yelled. "I'm just being realistic."

"Well, you just stand there and be realistic," Helaine snapped. "I'll fight this battle on my own." She stood up, and felt dizzy. She started to fall, but Byte grabbed her and helped her to stand.

"You can't fight *anything* in that state," she said, gently.

"I can because I must," Helaine repeated again. She shrugged off the helping hand, and started to walk toward the closet door.

"Oh, for heaven's sake!" Byte snapped. "Stay there before you fall down and break a bone or two. I'll get your stupid clothes!" She strode to the door and opened it. She felt inside, and pulled out the jeans and top Helaine had been wearing earlier. "Here!"

Helaine dressed in silence. By the time she had the clothes on, Byte had found her sneakers. Once she was fully dressed again, Helaine felt a little better. Certainly a little more confident—her gemstones were still in her jeans' pocket, and she could feel the strength flowing from them. "Now to get out of here."

There was only one other door in the room, obviously the one leading to the rest of the hospital. Unsurprisingly, it was locked.

Byte gave her a helpless look. "We can't get out that way," she said. "And there's no other exit."

"You will *never* learn to fight if all you see are losses," Helaine informed her. She reached out to touch her sapphire, which gave her the power of levitation. She could feel the magical strength inside her now, even if she was still physically pretty weak. "Stand aside from the door." Byte moved behind her, and Helaine felt the magic flow. She picked up the bed she'd been in, and flung it with all of her strength at the door. In a crash of splintering wood, the door collapsed. The bed slammed down amidst the wreckage, and Helaine stepped over it and into the corridor. She glanced back at Byte. "Are you coming with me to fight, or will you remain here and find more excuses for cowardice?"

"I am *not* a coward," Byte growled, joining her. "I'm a realist. I know we can't win." Then her voice softened. "But, unlike the doctors, I can't go along with what the Overmind commands."

"Good," Helaine said, approvingly. "I shall make a warrior of you yet. The first step is always to refuse to do what you know is evil, no matter how many good excuses you can find for giving in."

Byte looked surprised at the compliment. "I still think we're going to die," she explained. "But I'd rather be dead than making more slaves."

"We shall not die," Helaine said firmly. "And, even if we do, we die in a fight for right. What better death can there be than that?"

"Well, actually, I'd prefer not to die at all," Byte admitted.

"We all must die some day," Helaine said. "But it is our choice whether we die a warrior or a coward. You have chosen well."

She was leading the way down the corridor. As she'd suspected, they were in a hospital of sorts. She'd never been in one before herself, but both Score and Pixel had told her about them. They were supposed to be places where sick and injured people were healed. There were no such places on her home world, of course. On her world, medicine was mostly practiced by hedge-witches like Jenna. On Score's Earth, he had told her, it was a science.

But this was not a hospital for healing. Helaine felt her anger rising as they strode past rooms filled with babies. There were nurses looking after them, and most were surprisingly silent and peaceful. There were no parents around, because the Overmind considered them to be unnecessary. Babies would be taken from here to Houses of their own, and wired into the computers, which would see to their every need—even down to imaginary parents.

But before they left the hospital, each baby would be given a chip in his or her head . . .

Each of the babies in the nurseries had a small scar on their head, only about half an inch long . . . more slaves in the making, to feed the ego and ambition of the Overmind. This was evil, pure and simple, and Helaine would not allow it to continue as long as she had breath and strength.

And a mind of her own . . .

"Where do these chips come from?" she wondered aloud.

Byte shrugged. "They must be manufactured somewhere and shipped here," she suggested.

"Then there must be a store room for them here somewhere," Helaine said. "Let us find and destroy it."

"That won't do much," Byte protested. "The Overmind will simply have more shipped in."

"It will give these poor infants some time," Helaine said. "And perhaps we can destroy the Overmind before they are operated on. I think destroying the chips will be effective—though not as satisfying as it would be to chop off the hands of those wretched surgeons who implant them."

"You really have a lot of anger inside you, don't you?" Byte asked her.

"With so much evil in the world, how can I *not* be angry?" Helaine demanded.

A detached voice sounded in the air, as if from all around them. "Did you really think I would not be monitoring you?" the Overmind asked. "I cannot allow you to destroy the chips that I need."

"I had expected you to talk to us long before this," Helaine said, continuing her march onward. "Your monitoring changes nothing. You still need human hands to do your bidding, and these zombies you have nursing the babies cannot stop me."

"No, but my security guards can," the Overmind reminded her. "And they are guarding all possible targets for your anger. And more are on their way to take you into custody. I shall enjoy studying your magical powers. Magic intrigues me."

"And you appall me," Helaine answered. "I will not cooperate with you, no matter what force or persuasion you offer."

"That's very easy to say," the Overmind commented. "But you have no real idea of my strength. I could, for example, threaten to kill that girl with you. I have no need for her, but you seem to have formed some sort of emotional bond with her. Help me to control magic, or I shall have her killed."

Helaine stopped. She gave Byte a quick look, and knew that the girl was afraid. "Byte," she said, gently.

"If I do what the Overmind demands, many more innocent people will become its slaves. Would you wish me to save your life at such a price?"

"No," Byte said softly. Her eyes were brimming with tears. "I don't want to die, but I couldn't live with that on my conscience."

Helaine patted her encouragingly on the shoulder. "That is a truly brave decision. I take back whatever I said about you being a coward. You are a warrior." Byte looked a little more cheerful at that. Helaine glared at the air around them. "Your threat is meaningless, as you see. Byte would rather die than help you."

"She may not die," the Overmind answered. "She may simply lose her mind. She has an implant chip also, and I can take over her mind any time I so chose. Would you prefer that, Byte?"

"To lose my mind?" Byte shuddered. "No. But it is better than losing my soul by cooperating with you."

Helaine was right—the girl *was* a warrior at heart! "You have a brave heart," she said, approvingly.

"Do you think I wouldn't do it?" the Overmind asked.

"On the contrary," Helaine said, "I am certain that you *will* do it. Because you will never control her by force or persuasion—nor will you control me that way, either. We will both fight to defeat you while we have breath and minds of our own. You are able to take over our bodies, but that will be a weak and pointless victory for you, because if you do that, you will lose that which you want from us."

"There is a certain logic to your argument," the Overmind conceded. "But that logic is flawed. I cannot allow you to be a free agent, because then you would oppose my designs. So you will cooperate with me willingly, or I shall take over your minds. There is no third option."

Yes there is, Helaine thought. But it was not one the Overmind would understand—or approve of, if it did comprehend. Helaine simply needed time to work out the rough plan that was starting to take shape in her mind. But the Overmind was impatient, and hardly likely to give her that time. If only she could stall it somehow!

At that moment, two of the guards came around the bend of the corridor. Both held the pain tubes, and were prepared to fire. Helaine reached out with the aid of her chrysoprase, her power over the element of Earth. This enabled her to make the metal of the tubes rust and fall apart. The guards looked at their weapons as they literally turned to dust in their hands.

"I can do the same to you," Helaine informed them coldly. She didn't admit that she would never actually carry out that threat, of course. But these men didn't know that, and they hesitated, awaiting further instructions from the Overmind.

Which didn't come. "Fascinating," the Overmind commented. "Somehow this *magic* allowed you to accelerate a natural process, causing the weapons to decay."

Helaine grinned. "Intriguing, isn't it? And if you take over my mind, you'll never be able to harness that power."

"This is true," the Overmind agreed. "Perhaps it would be better to simply study your powers. I shall have you removed to an observation room, where your usage of magic will be monitored and analyzed."

"You're crazy if you think I'll agree to that," Helaine replied. Perfect! There would be a delay in the Overmind bringing further guards to subdue her. Meanwhile, she concentrated on her plan.

The Overmind had actually made a very serious error in implanting the chip in her mind. It was *supposed* to control her when the Overmind desired it, and otherwise to simply draw power for it from her mental abilities. But it was a *communications* device, connecting her mind to the Overmind! And her agate gave her the ability to control communications . . .

She felt out with her power to the chip in her brain. Then she tapped into the transmissions the chip was sending to the Overmind. Carefully, she probed the contact made, and she knew that she had gained access to the Overmind itself . . .

Now all that was needed was carefully applied magic.

She sent a burst of mental fire down the line of communications.

Instantly, the power in the hospital flickered. The two guards cried out, falling to their knees, clasping their heads in pain. Babies in the rooms around them started to scream. Nurses fell, crying out. Byte stared around, and then at Helaine.

"That's got to be you doing this," she gasped. "But how? And what are you doing?"

"Giving the Overmind a dose of its own medicine," Helaine said, smugly. "I'm giving it the pain it causes its slaves."

"And hurting those connected to it," Byte pointed out.

"I know that," Helaine admitted. "But it can't be helped. And it's only temporary. I'm just dealing out a lesson to the Overmind." She had stopped sending the power overload, and gradually everyone stopped screaming.

"What did you just do?" the Overmind demanded. "That was . . . a problem for my pathways."

"And there's more when I choose," Helaine informed it coldly. "I can do that to you any time I wish, and there is no way for you to stop it, since you made it possible through your implant chip. As long as you are linked to me, *I* am linked to *you*."

"You cannot be allowed to disrupt my command codes," the Overmind stated.

Helaine knew what would have to happen next, and so she was braced for the attack. The only way to safeguard itself was for the Overmind to take over her mind, even if it meant losing the ability to control magic. So it blasted her with the command to the chip to seize control of her mind.

But the command didn't work. Helaine was still controlling her communication with the Overmind, and she simply blocked the signal. Despite all of its powers, the Overmind *couldn't* take over her brain. She was locking it out.

There were still two problems with that, of course. First, it *could* still take control of Byte, but Helaine was gambling that, since the other girl was not an immediate threat, she would be safe for the moment. It looked like she was correct, because the Overmind was concentrating on taking over Helaine. The second problem was that the fight was draining a lot of her energy—and she didn't have a huge amount to begin with. She wouldn't be able to resist for very long.

But what other choice did she have? She had the power, but not the training to use the power to its best advantage. Nantor was stronger than she was, for example, because he'd been using magic for centuries. She was certain she was wasting a lot of energy unnecessarily, rather like a novice swimmer does while splashing about instead of swimming smoothly. But there was no way to change that.

"You are a more formidable foe than I had anticipated," the Overmind conceded. "But that does not mean that you can win this contest of wills. There is another way to remove you as a problem."

As Heleaine had feared, the Overmind had decided now to simply have her killed. If it sent guards with lethal weapons, then she would not be able to stop them. All her energies were taken in the mental fighting, and she could barely even focus on what was happening around her body.

But it turned out that her assumption was incorrect—the Overmind still did not want her dead; it wanted her controlled. And it did something she hadn't been expecting, and thus couldn't block.

It sent a command through the chip to contact Eremin.

Eremin! The dark, icy, evil self that she might one day become. The power that wished to take over her mind and body, as Nantor had possessed Pixel!

The one thing guaranteed to terrify Helaine . . .

And there was an answer almost immediately. Helaine could feel the chilling approach of Eremin, wakened from her sleep in the gem room of Jewel. Wakened, and ready to take possession of Helaine's heart and soul . . .

7

Pixel was finding that Nantor hadn't lied to him—he *was* getting weaker, and it was harder to keep his mind together. He knew that it was simply a matter of time now until he lost the battle, and he would simply dissipate and cease to exist, and Nantor would have control of his body completely. The only thing preventing this from happening was Pixel's determination not to allow Nantor to win, and his fears about what would happen to

Jenna if he did. Or what might have already happened to Jenna, of course. He knew from Nantor's thoughts that Jenna had simply been sent to Earth, along with Score and Dayta. But Jenna was a gentle innocent, and his own memories of Earth were that it could be a very dangerous place for someone like that.

But there was nothing he could do while he was imprisoned inside his own mind, and the "cell" was getting smaller every moment. Except, of course, to try and manipulate Nantor into helping people—which went completely against the grain for a monster like the magician. But he had seen the logic of Pixel's arguments and finally teamed up with Fargo and the other people here who were naturally immune to control by the Overmind.

As Nantor had complained—frequently!—it was a pitifully small number of people in all. Even waiting as long as they dared, they had only managed to recruit twenty-six immune Drones. "We can't possibly defeat the Overmind with such a pitiful force," Nantor raged. "Even with my magic thrown in. It is simply too powerful."

"You're forgetting a few things," Pixel informed him. "My friends."

"Score, Jenna, and Dayta are on the Earth," Nantor answered. "There is no way they can escape from there; they do not have the knowledge or control to conjure up a portal."

"You know, never learning to trust people has made your thinking really hazy," Pixel told him. "You don't have a clue as to their abilities—or *their* friends. There *is* a way for them to escape from the Earth and to return here, but I won't tell you what it is. Suffice it to say that if they *can* get off the Earth, then they *will*. I have no doubt of that. They may already be back here. And, besides that, Helaine is already inside the Administration Building."

"As a prisoner," Nantor pointed out. "She will have been neutralized or killed by now. We can look for no help from her."

"Would Eremin be dead by now?" Pixel demanded.

"No, but she is as strong as I am—and even more ruthless."

"And Helaine is strong, too—and very, very determined." Pixel knew he was guilty of wishful thinking, but he had to press on. "When we get inside the building, we may already find allies."

"I doubt it," Nantor said, with conviction. "However, we have no choice in the matter. If I am to rule

the Diadem again, I cannot allow this Overmind creature to survive. It is far too dangerous and determined
a foe. Now that it knows that portals are possible, it
will not rest until it knows how to construct them."

That wasn't the reason Pixel wanted the Overmind
destroyed, but Nantor certainly did have a point. An
Overmind with the power to move to other worlds
would be a horrendous monster, worse than it already
was. "Then let's go and kick some computer butt," he
said.

Nantor gestured to Fargo and the others. At the
head of his small, pitiful army, he marched back to the
Administration Building. To Pixel's—and Nantor's—
surprise, they were not met by any resistance. Puzzled,
they moved inside the foyer. There were plenty of
people there, and many of them were guards, clearly
intended to stop Nantor's band. But they were not in
any condition to fight—they were all writhing on the
ground, howling and clutching their heads.

"Most peculiar," Nantor commented. He wasn't at
all concerned about the pain these victims were un-
dergoing. "Perhaps I was too hasty in dismissing the
possibility that your friends might be helpful. It is
clearly some enemy of the Overmind doing this."

That was clear enough, but even Pixel didn't have a clue as to who could be doing this, or how. He wasn't going to admit that to Nantor, though—let the fiend think it was part of Pixel's scheme! "We need to make sure that these people can't recover and fight us one we've moved on," he said.

Nantor started to gather power. "I can kill them without much problem."

"No!" Pixel cried. "There's no need to kill them." He was appalled at how casually Nantor had suggested such a horrible thing. How could this monster have ever grown out of him? What could have ever changed Pixel into Nantor? He thought quickly. "They're only a problem if the Overmind can control them. Ask Fargo if anyone in her group can use the equipment here to set up a radio dampening field, and block all signals from the Overmind to its slaves." He grinned mentally as he thought of a good argument. "If you just kill these people, the Overmind will call in more troops. But if there's a dampening field in here, then *anyone* the Overmind brings in will be lost."

"A good point," Nantor conceded. He discussed Pixel's idea with Fargo and the others. Some of the men knew electronics, and two of them were certain they could rig up a dampening field in a matter of minutes.

"Fine," Nantor decided. "Stay here and do it." He gestured. "You five, collect weapons from fallen guards, and stay here to make certain nobody can interfere with them as they work. The rest of us will press on."

Pixel was impressed—Nantor's idea was workable, and should guard their backs. "But why move on?" he asked. "We can access the Overmind from anywhere in this building."

Nantor's response was filled with scorn. "Because he has Helaine captive, and planned to implant a chip in her head. If he has controlled her, he may already have access to portal creation. I have to be certain that this is not the case. Also, I too need Helaine—to bring back Eremin. Magic is still in a state of rupture in the Diadem, and I need to fix it. That means travelling to Jewel. But if I go there alone, I will be trapped by the power—there must be at least two magicians if one is to escape."

"You're planning to sacrifice Eremin so you can be free?" Pixel asked. "Boy, I knew that you Three Who Rule were pretty nasty, but that's bad, even for you."

"Jewel must be stabilized, or the Diadem will descend into chaos," Nantor replied. "Only a magician can control the power there, but it traps whoever controls it. I will not be held captive again, not when there are worlds where I can conquer and rule. Eremin will become the captive, not me."

"And what about Traxis?" asked Pixel.

"If I have Eremin, I do not need him. He can stay trapped, forever. And to ensure that he is, I shall go to Earth after Jewel and destroy Score, so Traxis can never escape."

"You've thought it out pretty well, haven't you?" Pixel asked, bitterly. "But what if Eremin won't cooperate with your plan? If you bring her back, *she* may plan to use *you*."

"I'm sure she would," Nantor agreed. "But she won't get the chance. I do not intend to restore her to corporeal form until I reach Jewel. Then she will have no chance to plot in advance."

"You'll simply bring her back, and then trap her again," Pixel finished. "Nasty, but effective, I suppose. But first we have to find Helaine."

"Which is simplicity itself," Nantor answered. He held Pixel's ruby in his hand. "After all, one of our skills is locating things and people." He concentrated a moment, and a red line of light led off into the building. "Let us go and find your friend."

He led the remaining forces through the building. They passed from offices into an area that was clearly a hospital. The rooms seemed to be filled with crying babies and howling nurses. Pixel had to steel himself against their pitiful cries.

"Where the implants are done," Fargo growled. "A filthy process, aided by traitors to their own people. It must be stopped."

"It will be, once the Overmind is destroyed," Nantor informed her. "Your people will be free." *Until I enslave them*, he added to himself. Pixel clearly heard the thought. He wasn't sure which would be the greater of the two monsters.

They finally reached a corridor where there were people still standing. Pixel was almost deliriously happy to see that they were Helaine and Byte, though both looked very tired and drained. He wondered what was happening, but he didn't have control over his own mouth to ask questions. He had to rely on Nantor instead.

"So, child," Nantor growled at Helaine. "You are still alive."

Helaine turned very cold, pain-filled eyes onto him. "Nantor," she said, scornfully. "You always were a fool. Can't you tell the difference between a child and a woman?"

Nantor blinked, and stared at her. "Eremin?"

"Eremin," Helaine said firmly. "This idiot computer has resurrected me, and is attacking me in my own mind."

Pixel would have gone pale if he had control over his body. Eremin! Then Helaine was as trapped in her own mind as he was in his own. He'd already failed her . . .

Nantor, on the other hand, was delighted. Not because he *liked* Eremin, of course, but because he *needed* her, and aimed to betray her. He smiled, cheerfully. "It's nice to have you back again."

Helaine's body gave his a cold stare. "You were always a poor liar," she snapped. "You're no more glad to see me than I am to see you. But we need one another at this moment, so I suggest we set aside our differences and deceits."

"Same old Eremin," Nantor commented. "Ever the icy witch."

"Let's get on with it," she answered. "We have two main problems to face. First, this irritating computer program; second, the dissolution of magic due to our being freed from the Diadem Analog."

"Agreed," Nantor said. "I think we had better not leave this Overmind behind us to try and attack us once we move on. It is surpisingly intelligent and adaptive."

"True," Eremin replied. "But I have it temporarily in trouble. It was foolish enough to give me access to its own programming, and I have been using that to attack it. But it must be isolated from the rest of its operating system, and I need your skills for that."

Nantor gave her a suspicious glare. "You seem to suddenly know a lot about computers, considering your background."

Eremin sighed. "And you aren't *listening* to me. I *told* you, it gave me access to it through a communications device. I drained some information from it before it managed to clamp down on the link and fight me."

"There's no need to get surly," Nantor complained. "All that time in suspension hasn't improved you, has it?"

"No more than it's made you more intelligent," Eremin sniped. "Are we going to get on with it, or do you wish to stand here and trade insults while the Diadem falls apart around us?"

"All right," Nantor agreed. "What did you have in mind?"

"I have access to the Overmind through the link in the chip he placed in this head," Eremin explained, tapping herself. "What we need to do is to download the portion of the programming that contains its personality into this chip."

"Oh, yes?" Nantor asked suspiciously. "And when you have the Overmind in your head and in your control, you'll do *what* with it?"

"Don't be so suspicious," Eremin growled. "We then go to Jewel. The problem with the Diadem Analog is that *you're* missing from the gem that controls Calomir, and that's what's throwing everything out of order."

"I know I'm missing," Nantor agreed. "So what?"

Eremin glared at him. "Either you've become stupider through too long a captivity, or else that boy you've replaced was a whole lot smarter than you. I'm sure *he* would understand my plan."

Yes, I would, Pixel thought to himself. And, as far as he could see, it should work brilliantly. Eremin, it seemed, was a lot smarter than Helaine. Poor Helaine! Was she as trapped in her own mind as he was in his? Or had she already been destroyed? Try as he might, he couldn't see any way out of this for either of them, even if Eremin and Nantor would have to save the Diadem—in order to rule it.

"I think you've become more of a shrew than ever," Nantor complained. "Stop playing games, and just tell me what you have in mind."

Pixel was suddenly aware of something that almost made him forget his problems. Nantor *wasn't* him! He couldn't be, because *he* could see Eremin's plan quite simply, and Nantor couldn't. It wasn't simply a matter of Nantor being better trained in magic, and having forgotten other matters. Nantor's brain simply didn't work the same way that Pixel's did.

So I'm safe from ever really turning into Nantor, Pixel thought, ironically. *But I'm doomed to be thrown out of my own body anyway.* But it was an immense relief to know that, no matter what happened, he could never turn into Nantor. They truly were two completely separate people. And the same undoubtedly held true for Helaine and Score as well. Maybe once they had managed to grow up into Eremin and Traxis, but they would never do that now. They were already far too different from the way the Three had once been ever to be doomed to follow that path again.

Eremin sighed. "We download the Overmind from the chip in my head into your abandoned crystal. The Overmind is quite legitimately a life form from Calomir, so downloading it will serve to repower the gem, and reconstruct the Diadem Analog. The flow of magic will be healed—and *neither* of us has to stay behind on Jewel to keep it in shape."

Pixel could feel the understanding flooding belatedly through Nantor's mind. He had worked all of this out as Eremin had suggested the plan, but it had taken Nantor a lot longer to reach the same conclusion.

"That's actually a very good plan," Nantor agreed. "And certainly workable."

"Of course it is," Eremin said coldly. "Now, stop dragging this out, and let's get to work. I want this chip out of my head as soon as possible, and magic restored. I'm getting a headache, and you *know* how I get when I have a headache."

"Yes—nastier than normal." Nantor quite clearly didn't want to experience that again. It appeared he'd been on the receiving end of some of Eremin's temper tantrums in the past. "All right, focus."

Nantor concentrated, and Pixel could feel the flow of magic. He could use the jacinth himself to call things to him, but not with the strength and power that Nantor could apply. Eremin gave a cry, and her knees started to buckle. Byte grabbed her to help her steady herself.

"Get your hands off me, child," Eremin snarled, pushing the startled Byte aside. "I don't require your assistance."

Nantor chuckled, glad that someone other than him was feeling the edge of Eremin's notorious temper. "Concentrate," he admonished her. "This is quite tricky. The Overmind is fighting me, and it is quite powerful—and large. I'm having to strip it to its core to enable it to fit inside the chip."

"Just get on with it, instead of making excuses," Eremin complained. She was steadying herself against a wall, and rubbing her temples. "I want it out of my head. Having two of us in here already is quite bad enough."

Two! Pixel felt elated. So Helaine was still alive—but, like him, trapped. She could still be restored, then. But his spirits slumped. *How* could she be restored? There was nothing that he could do. And both Score and Jenna were gone. Even if they were here, how could either of them stand up to two of the Three Who Ruled?

It was looking more and more like they were in a trap that this time there was no way to get out of without help that simply wasn't going to come.

Nantor started to use his magic; once again, Pixel could almost grasp what he was doing and how he was doing it. But it was magic born out of hundreds of years of practice, and he knew he wouldn't be able to duplicate it for a long, long time yet. However, it was very effective. The Overmind was being blocked from controlling any of his puppets by Helaine—no *Eremin*—and it simply couldn't stand up to Nantor's magic. Pixel could *feel* the living computer entity being stripped and squeezed, and then it was finally gone, concentrated into the chip that lay in Helaine's head.

"You have no idea how much this hurts," Eremin growled through clenched teeth. "Let's get to Jewel *now*."

Nantor nodded, and started to cast the spell that would create the necessary portals. Even for someone with Nantor's skills, it wasn't possible to move to Jewel in just one jump—he had to move from layer to layer in the Diadem to reach the center.

Meanwhile, Byte was looking very confused. "What is happening?" she asked. She gestured around. Some of the security guards were still comatose, but others were starting to awaken. "Should I use the pain guns on them?"

"There will be no need," Nantor told her. "They are no longer being controlled by the Overmind. They have their own wills back."

"But some are still unconscious," Byte protested. "Why aren't they all?"

Nantor hated the distraction, but answering the idiot's questions seemed to be the quickest way to shut her up. "It all depends on how long they were under its influence. The newer ones still possess some will and mind of their own. The older ones have had it all drained from them. They'll be drooling idiots until they die."

"So," Fargo said, "the rebellion worked? We're free?"

Nantor gave her a nasty grin. "For now. The Overmind is gone, and won't be back. But *we* shall be back, and the Three Who Rule will take over the Diadem again. Enjoy your freedom—for the short time it lasts." With a gesture, he brought the portal into being. "Come," he said to Eremin. "It is time for us to return to our rightful places, as the supreme rulers of the Diadem!"

8

Jenna stared at Shanara, initially in shock, and then in anger. "How can Score be dead?" she demanded. "He was with us when we stepped into the portal. He should have been right behind us."

"This pair did something," Dayta said, with absolute conviction. "They've got guilt written all over their faces."

She was right; Jenna could see the truth on Shanara's troubled, twisted features. "You betrayed him?" she asked, incredulously. "He *trusted* you, and you *betrayed* him?"

"You don't understand," Shanara said, wringing her hands helplessly. "We had no choice."

"You're right," Jenna agreed. "I *don't* understand. But you'd better make me understand, or you are going to be very, very sorry." Normally, Jenna was a quiet, loving person, but she had been through too much. Pixel—the boy she loved—might well be dead by now. And Score, the only other boy who'd ever treated her like a *person*, might also have been killed. By his friends. Her normally pleasant nature was getting buried under a mountain of rage. "I don't care if you *are* a magician, you'll find out what I'm capable of."

Dayta laid a hand on her arm, trying to calm her. "Let's take it step by step," she suggested. She turned to Shanara. "Okay, *what*, exactly, happened to Score? Where is he?"

"On a world called Hatrill," Shanara said, miserably. "A place he can't possibly survive."

"Why not?" Dayta demanded.

"Because it's filled with killer plants," Shanara said. "All they do is attack and devour anything that moves. So the moment he arrived, he'd have been under attack. By now he must be dead."

"I think you seriously underestimate his capabilities," Jenna said, furiously. "And if you haven't, then you'd better not underestimate mine. He can't be dead. Now, form another portal to Hatrill *immediately*."

"I can't," Shanara said. "It takes too much energy from me. I won't be able to do it for several hours."

Oracle stepped forward. He looked just as troubled as Shanara, but resolved.

"To rescue Score is a noble cause;

"But I beg of you to use this pause.

"Understand our reasons and our fear,

"And why he may never return here."

"You *traitor*," Jenna spat. "You're just trying to delay me to make certain he's killed."

"I don't think they're lying," Dayta offered. "I'm sure we'd be able to tell if they were."

"Well, *I* can be sure." Jenna turned to Shanara, and exerted all of her power of persuasion. "You will tell me only the truth," she commanded. "Can the portal be formed?"

"Not for several hours," the magician answered, and Jenna knew she was speaking the truth.

"Very well, then," Jenna said. "I will accept this. But as soon as you can form a portal, you *will* do so. Do you understand me?"

"Yes." Shanara's shoulders slumped, wearily. defeated. "But he *will* be dead. Nobody could survive that hellish place for more than a half hour."

"We'll see about that," Jenna said firmly. "And you had better pray that you are wrong. Pixel may already be dead, and if you've caused us to lose Score as well, my restraint will be frayed completely through."

Dayta touched her arm again. "Enough," she suggested. "I understand your anger and your pain, but it will do you no good to brood. Besides, this pair claims they had good reasons to try and kill Score—maybe we should listen to them?"

Jenna was very little in the mood to be reasonable right now—she was worried sick about both Pixel and Score. But the words sank in finally, and she nodded, numbly. "All right," she agreed, turning to Shanara. "*You* explain." She glared at Oracle. "I don't think my patience will be aided by his use of really bad poetry."

All the fight seemed to have fled Shanara. She collapsed into a chair. Jenna noticed for the first time that the magician's magical partner Blink, the lazy red panda, was missing. Was it possible he was up to something behind their backs. "Where's Blink?" she asked.

"Sleeping, as always," Shanara said listlessly. "Our complex spell of the portal wore him out. And it's because of the complexity that we can't make another portal too soon. We had to set the portal spell so that it caught only Score, Helaine, or Pixel. We had no wish to harm you." She glanced at Dayta. "Or anyone else. The trap was only for the three of them."

"But *why?*" Jenna cried. "You two were supposed to be their good friends."

"Of Score, Helaine, and Pixel, we are good friends and true, but the same cannot be said of the likes of you-know-who," Oracle offered.

"You cannot understand," Shanara said. "You can never understand the horror, because you lived on a Rim World. You were spared the reign of the Three Who Rule. But the rest of the Diadem was not so fortunate. If they had not quarreled and then got themselves virtually killed, they would have spread their evil to your worlds. The Three . . ." She clutched for words. "They had power, more power than you can imagine. They tapped the source of magic on Jewel, and could use it almost without limit. Their every whim was law for millions of inhabitants of the Diadem. Nobody could stand up to them. Whatever they wanted, they took. If anyone displeased them, that person was killed in the most horrific of tortures." Shanara looked up.

"You must have noted that I change my appearance from day to day."

Jenna shrugged. "You are the Magician of Illusion. It's just a game you play, isn't it?"

"No game." Shanara shuddered. "I displeased Traxis, and he . . . punished me." She gestured at her face, her long, lime-green hair, and shapely body. "This is how I once looked, but no longer do. It took him a long time to change me from this, and he enjoyed every moment of it. You can have no idea the pain I endured—and the further pain I will endure if Traxis should ever be reborn."

"Show me," Jenna ordered.

Shanara shook her head. "I have never allowed my illusion to lapse since this was done to me. No one but Traxis has ever seen what I now look like."

"Show me," Jenna ordered, mercilessly. If she was to understand Shanara's betrayal, she had to *know*. She exerted all of the force of her power of persuasion. "Show me!"

Shanara, weakened already by guilt and self-doubt, could not stand up to Jenna's power. She let the illusion fade away.

Both Jenna and Dayta fell back, crying out in horror.

Shanara's face was a mass of scar tissue. There was almost no inch of her skin untouched. Her left eye was almost blind, and her mouth curled in a permanent sneer. Parts of her arms were visible, and they showed the same horrific evidence of terrible torture. Shanara restored the illusion, and smiled gently.

"Now you see the reason for my illusions," she murmured.

"Traxis did *that* to you?" Jenna gasped, still almost choking from the memory of the sight.

"Yes. He spent a long, long time at it. It was . . . an excruciating experience, one that I try to forget as much as possible."

"I can see why you would," Dayta agreed. "But why would he do anything so horrible to you?"

"Because I had the courage to stand up to the Three and to tell them that what they were doing was wrong." Shanara sighed. "I could not stand by and see them pillaging and murdering and do nothing. I tried to fight them, but my powers were too weak. They chose Traxis to do this to me as a punishment—both to me and to him. I was closer to him that to anyone, and he was forced to prove that he was more loyal to them than to me. And he gave every indication that he enjoyed what he did." She shook her head slightly.

"So I think you can understand why I would do almost anything to ensure that the Three can *never* return to power. Even if that means killing Score, Helaine, and Pixel in the process."

"I can understand your pain and your fear," Jenna said. "But you still acted badly. Score is *not* Traxis, and most likely never will be. There is no evidence of any of this dreadful cruelty in him."

"That isn't the point!" Shanara exclaimed. "Don't you understand? Score's body is also the body that *can* host Traxis. Perhaps the current Score won't become Traxis—having known both of them, I can quite readily agree that they are very, very different people. But Traxis still exists—he is imprisoned inside a gemstone on Jewel, but his personality is intact. If it can reinhabit Score's body, then Traxis will live again. That was the original plan of the Three, and they haven't given up on it."

Dayta looked puzzled. "Then why kill *Score?* Why not Traxis?"

"It's not that simple," Shanara explained. "For one thing, Traxis's personality is helping to keep the Diadem Analog working. If I were to kill him, then I should have to imprison some other soul from Earth to take his place. But that's not the only reason. The other is that Traxis is on Jewel—and it would kill me if I even attempted to pass through a portal to that planet. The magical power is so intense there that only the strongest of magic-users can survive there. I'm only a second-rate magician, and the power flux would fry me alive. So I have no option—it's Score or nothing."

"It's still a terrible betrayal of people who trust you," Jenna said.

"Do you think I don't know that?" Shanara cried in anguish. "I would never have done it, except for the fact that Nantor is already back. One of the Three is dangerous enough—but perhaps he can be killed by the rest of us. Two would be virtually impossible to defeat, and all Three . . ." She shook her head. "We would be doomed. No matter what the personal cost—and you can have no idea how hard it was for me to agree to killing Score—I *cannot* allow the Three to return."

Jenna was struggling to understand all of this. "You're right, I *don't* know what evils the Three committed. I didn't live through them, thankfully. And perhaps they would be even worse if they return. But they *haven't* returned yet, and they may never do so. Nantor is inhabiting Pixel's body, it's true, but we don't know that Pixel is dead. Nor do we know that we can't eject Nantor and restore Pixel. And until I know that Pixel is definitely dead, I'm not going to give up on him." She reached out to grip Shanara's hands. "I know you've suffered much, and I understand that you feel that what you did was called for. But you're *wrong*. Killing any of your friends is the wrong way to prevent a disaster. Hasn't it occurred to you that if Score somehow survives this betrayal of yours, it might be this very betrayal that could push him over the edge and *make* him into Traxis? You may not be saving the Diadem by your actions, but condemning it."

Dayta nodded her agreement. "I know I probably don't have any right to speak here—I'm not a magic user, and I know I'm kind of young. But there's one thing that's quite clear to me—you can't fight evil with evil. Killing Score is evil, even if you're doing it to prevent what you see as a greater evil." She shrugged. "I'll shut up now."

Shanar shook her head. "No, you're right. What I did was *wrong*. I have been allowing my fears—both for myself and others—to rule my actions. Even if I can somehow justify it to myself, it's still wrong."

"Then we'd better work together and see if we can correct it," Jenna said decisively. "Enough recriminations and explanations. What we need now is to try and save Score. He's resourceful and tough, and if anyone can survive Hatrill's perils, it's him. But the longer he's there, the more danger he's in. We need to open a portal there, and get him off, if we can."

"But I'm still not strong enough to attempt it," Shanara protested.

"You forget," Jenna reminded her, "that I am a magician, too. And stronger than you are. And I'm a healer, and I can give you strength. If we work together on this, I believe we can form a portal and save Score."

Shanara looked hopeful. "Yes, you're right—I was giving in to despair again. Very well, let's go and get Blink, and see if the two of us together can't work miracles." She strode off, fresh determination in her steps.

Jenna followed along, hoping that she wasn't being foolish. She knew it was most likely that Score was already dead. And if he was—what then? She didn't know. Losing a friend like him would be a hard blow, and it would be compounded if Pixel were also dead.

Stop that! she ordered herself. She *had* to believe there was a chance.

The problem was that her powers of persuasion only worked on other people—and not herself.

9

Score sat huddled miserably in his small cave. He couldn't light a fire, because there was no dead wood to burn. *Everything* on this planet was eaten. He could create a magical fire, of course, or even use his powers to turn a stone into coal, which would burn. But he didn't dare use any of his strength for that. He knew that as soon as the sun rose, the killer plants would return to carnivorous life and start hunting him again.

Why had Shanara and Oracle done this to him? He couldn't understand it, but he promised himself vengeance on them just as soon as he had a chance. He'd trusted them, almost loved them, and they had betrayed him. He had been right all along—trusting people was a game for idiots. Being a loner was the only safe way to live.

Only . . . he was more worried for Helaine than he was for himself, if that were possible. Okay, she was a strong, courageous warrior, but there were things she couldn't combat. He felt as if he were betraying her by not being there to help her. Pixel, too, of course—he was very fond of that naive nitwit—and Jenna. But Helaine was the one he was most scared for.

Why? She was just a girl, and often a very annoying one. Pretty, of course, and brave, and sometimes the most fun to be with. But she was so irritating, with her insistence on honor and bravery, and her almost total lack of a sense of humor. She'd be fine without him. He should be worrying about himself, not her. She, at least, had friends with her to help—he was all alone, betrayed, and dumped here to die.

Nobody cared about him, and there was no one to help him.

The air in front of him puckered, growing darker even in this gloomy night.

A portal!

Score didn't care where it might lead—even into worse danger, if that was possible—he just wanted off this killer planet! He jumped to his feet and dove through the gateway before it closed behind him.

He emerged to find himself inside Shanara's castle, the familiar room littered with books and magical apparatus. Blink sat on the table, yawning as if he'd done a year's hard work. Oracle stood in the background, as if trying to avoid being seen. Shanara and Jenna—both looking exhausted—stood close by. That girl from Pixel's planet, Dayta, was behind them, her eyes wide with astonishment.

He was wrong—he *wasn't* without friends.

He grabbed Jenna and hugged her tightly. "Thank you!" he gasped. "You have no idea how glad I am to be off that planet."

"You're welcome," Jenna answered, his face lit with delight. "It is such a relief to find you're still alive. Some of us," and she looked at Shanara, "were sure you were dead."

"And I almost was," Score agreed. His relief at being rescued was now being drowned by his anger. "As you planned," he growled. He could feel the build-up in his magical power now he had crossed into an inner ring of the Diadem. Fueled by anger, he knew he could take Shanara down without much of a fight. Especially since she didn't seem to be raising any of her own defenses.

The anger had grown, almost filling him. She had betrayed him, and the only way to deal with that kind of scum was to eradicate it. He reached out for the power, preparing to blast her into tiny fragments.

"No, Score!" Jenna said firmly, stepping between them. "This isn't the right way."

"Get out of the way, Jenna," he warned her. "That lady's got some major payback coming." He started to form a fireball.

"And what are you going to do?" Jenna asked him, unmoving. "Kill her? Is that what you want? Or is it your anger speaking? Is it your inner Traxis speaking?"

Traxis? What was she talking about? Score couldn't understand what she was saying for a moment. "Get out of the way," he repeated.

"No." Jenna crossed her arms and stood firm. "If you want to kill her, you'll have to kill me first."

"If that's the way you want it," Score agreed. He was astonished—Jenna wasn't even trying to use her power of persuasion on him. He knew she could stop him if she wanted to. So why wasn't she trying?

Because, he realized, she knew that stopping him by magic wouldn't be the real answer. It might work in the short term, but not for very long. The only way she could stop him was to convince him honestly to stop. "I don't want to hurt you," he told her. "You know that."

"I'm relying on it," Jenna replied. But she did look relieved.

"Then why are you protecting her?" he demanded, pointing at Shanara.

"Because you don't *really* want to kill her," Jenna said. "That's just temporary anger that you're listening to. Yes, Shanara dumped you on that world to kill you—but only because she thought she had no choice." She turned to Shanara. "Show him."

"No," Shanara whispered. "No, not *him*. I dare not."

"Show him!" Jenna insisted. But she was still not using magic to enforce her will. "As long as you hide from him, there will only be mistrust, anger, and fear between you. Show him!"

Score didn't have a clue what was going on here, but he fought to keep his anger in check. Jenna was right—deep down, he didn't really want to kill Shanara. He knew he was simply lashing out. But that didn't mean his feelings weren't real, or that the danger he'd give in to his murderous fury wasn't quite close to happening. But he was struggling to keep it in check.

Shanara was one of the most beautiful people he'd even seen. But he also knew that Shanara was projecting an illusion, and that she might look like anything from a six-year-old child to a thousand-year-old hag.

He wasn't at all prepared for what he saw when she dropped the illusion. Thankfully, she didn't drop it for long, because he felt sick at what he saw. Scarring all over a once beautiful body, wounds that had to hurt her clear down to the bone.

"Are you . . . in pain?" he asked her, shaking at what he'd seen.

"Not any more," Shanara replied. "Magic can help with much of it."

He was starting to understand, but he was forced to ask the next question. "Who did that to you?"

"Traxis."

The one word cut him almost as deeply as her scars. He wasn't Traxis—but he *might* be. If he'd given in to his anger and fried Shanara, then he would have been well on the road to becoming Traxis. He felt almost physically sick at this realization. He turned to Jenna. "Thank you," he said, honestly. "For stopping me."

"I'd like to think you'd have stopped yourself," she replied, with a half-smile.

"I'd like to think so, too," he agreed. "But we both know it wouldn't have been true. I needed a good friend to refuse to let me be the worst I can be."

"Then let's be the best," Jenna suggested. "You're safe, we're together again, and we have our power back. Don't you think it's time to go and save Pixel, Helaine, and a planet?"

Score grinned. "Girl, you rock," he told her approvingly. He looked over at Shanara and the still-silent Oracle. "You know, I think that Jenna would be able to stop us from becoming the Three, even if we couldn't stop ourselves. She's some girl, isn't she?"

"She is indeed," Shanara agreed. "But she's also correct—you have a battle to return to. If it is possible, Pixel needs to be saved. If it isn't—well, the Diadem will need rescuing again. But shouldn't you be fixing the problem with magic first?"

"We need Nantor to do that," Score said. "I've been thinking about it—the Analog is broken because he's out of it. The only way to make it whole again is to imprison him there once more. So our first task has to be to capture him. That means returning to Calomir again." Score sighed. "I always try to avoid work, but it does have a way of creeping up on me. Okay, fire up the portal to Calomir—we've got a world or two to rescue." He winked at Jenna, and then reached out a hand for Dayta. "Come on, you'd better go back with us. You can't stay here."

"I want to be home," she agreed. "If there's fighting to be done, that's my planet in danger."

"Good girl." Score nodded to Shanara, who gathered all of her strength to form another portal. "No tricks?" he asked her.

"Never again," she promised.

"Good." To show he believed her, Score stepped through the portal first. He thought he was ready for anything, but he was wrong. He was certainly not expecting to appear in a nursery filled with crying babies. Jenna and Dayta were just as surprised when they came through the portal, which closed behind them. Score looked around the room, and saw a familiar face.

"Fargo!" he called. "What's going on? Where's the battle?"

"It's over," Fargo said, but she didn't sound at all happy. She was directing anyone she could find to help with the infants. "And it's left us a lot of problems."

"Can I help?" Dayta asked.

"Indeed you can," Fargo answered. "There are several hundred babies all crying for food. It used to be automated, but with the Overmind gone, we have to start doing things by hand. It's overwhelming."

"Gone?" Score was completely confused by now. "What have we missed?"

"That Pixel, or Nantor, or whoever he is, teamed up with Helaine. They somehow managed to get the Overmind out of the computer system, which left all controls dead. Half the people who have chips in their heads have gone comatose, and the others are slowly recovering their wits. All the systems that the Overmind ran have shut down, and now we've got thousands of people needing immediate help. The whole planet is falling into chaos."

"That tends to happen when people have to start thinking for themselves," Score agreed. "Quick suggestion—if the computers are down, then that means all of the kids in their virtual reality worlds out there are starting to wake up. You'll have a lot of people who can help you if you can start organizing them." He pointed to Dayta. "I think she'll be able to start handling their recruitment."

"Yes," Fargo agreed, looking relieved. "That will be a huge help. We're in such a mess now, I hardly know where to start."

"It's your planet again," Jenna told her. "You have to work it out."

"And we have our own troubles, or we'd help," Score said. "Where are Nantor and Helaine now?"

"They vanished through one of those gaps in the air you magicians keep making," Fargo said. "And he was calling Helaine by a different name. Hairy-something."

Score went cold. "Eremin?"

"That's it."

"Oh, no." He stared bleakly at Jenna. "Helaine's been possessed as well; that's two of the Three back now. They must have gone on the Jewel to try and fix the source of magic. We haven't any option but to follow them."

"Two against two now?" Jenna asked, pale.

"But those two are going to be much stronger together than the two of us," Score told her. "I have a horrible feeling we're going to get creamed. But we have to try it, because we dare not allow them to stay there with all that power available to them."

"Isn't there a risk that they'll bring Traxis back in you?" Jenna asked.

"I doubt it," Score said. "The Three never did get along, and there's no reason that the pair of them would need to bring Traxis back. No, I think it's much more likely that they'll just kill the pair of us. Then they'll start taking over the Diadem again. What we need is a sneaky weapon . . ."

Fargo gave them a bleak smile. "I have a suggestion," she said. "Those two magicians don't know much about science, do they?"

"No, they don't," Score agreed. He gave the woman a lopsided grin. "You're right—what we need is something nonmagical but effective."

Fargo went to a cabinet, and pulled out several items. "Try these," she suggested. Two of the items were hypodermic needles, filled with a cloudy liquid. "Nantor promised to return here and conquer us, so I thought I'd better get ready for him. Tranquilizers, that will act almost instantly." She added two pain guns to them. "And a bit of fire-power won't hurt."

"Right." Score and Jenna both pocketed one of each item. "We're going to do our best to beat Nantor and Eremin. But it's still possible that we'll lose. If either of them—or either of us, for that matter—come back here, expect the worst. None of us may be ourselves."

"Then let's set up a password," Fargo suggested. "How about *template*? If you don't say that, we'll assume the worst and fight."

"Good plan," Score agreed. He turned to Jenna. "Are you ready for this? There's an awfully good chance we won't live through the next hour."

"I have to try and save Pixel," Jenna said, simply. "And you have to save Helaine. What choice does either of us have?"

"None at all, as usual." Score concentrated, and linked his mind with Shanara's. "Okay," he told her, "it's traveling time again . . ."

This was it. The final battle. If he and Jenna were to survive, they had to fight two of the most powerful magicians ever. And armed only with their wits, feeble powers, and a handful of weapons. Score honestly didn't give much for their chances. But, as Jenna had said, what other option did they have?

10

Helaine didn't know how much longer she could keep going. Her mind felt like it was on fire, and her body was almost exhausted. It had taken Nantor two attempts to create the final portal that had brought them finally to Jewel. Here, the power was more intense, but at the same time, it was badly *twisted*, which was also contributing to her problems.

The stone walls of the castle that the Three Who Rule had used were as they had been when she, Score, and Pixel had left here more than a year ago. The inner room where the Analog lay was still locked and sealed with the unicorn horn that Thunder had given them.

"Are you all right?" Nantor asked her, sharply, glaring at her.

"Of course I'm not all right!" Helaine yelled. "I've now got *three* minds inside my head, you moron. Let's get on with it!" Actually, that wasn't true—there were only two in there, and the Overmind was pretty much sealed off and isolated in the chip. Despite what she'd told Nantor, Eremin was not in charge.

In fact, Helaine had managed to block her completely. Her power of communication had been strong enough to prevent Eremin from seizing control, but she knew that she didn't dare let Nantor know it. He was only going along with her plan to recharge the Analog because he thought it was Eremin's idea. There was no way he'd cooperate with mere Helaine. And it was getting simpler all the time to pretend to be Eremin—all she had to do was to act with utter contempt and selfishness, and that was, sadly, all too easy for her.

Turning into Eremin was the possibility that scared her more than anything else in her life. She knew the potential was within her, and play-acting Eremin had shown her how frighteningly possible it would be for her to succumb. Except that, of course, she had no intention of ever becoming that icy, haughty witch. It had not been easy for her, but Helaine had struggled to become warm and human.

"There's no need to be so nasty," Nantor complained. He appeared to be completely taken in by Helaine's acting. "We're almost there. Once we're inside the inner room, we only have to download the Overmind into my old gemstone, and then things will start to heal. You'll feel better then."

"Then let's get on with it," Helaine growled. She walked unsteadily to the door, and removed the unicorn horn. This had the power to contain and negate magic, and neither of them dared to handle it for long. It would drain them of their powers almost completely. She set it carefully aside, not wanting to damage it. There was already a large crack in it, and there was no way to know how long it would last.

Nantor pushed open the door to the inner room, laughing. "Come, Eremin," he called. "Now we can reclaim our heritage!"

Helaine stumbled into the room behind him. For a moment, her breath was taken from her as she stared at the Analog once more.

It hung suspended in the air by magic—a detailed map of the Diadem. Each world was represented by a single immense gemstone, all at least the size of her fist. All but one of the jewels was glowing with an inner light. Each gem contained the life-essence of some inhabitant of the world that the gem stood for; only the one for Calomir was dark and lifeless, and it was this that was throwing the balance of magic so off-kilter. Nantor had been imprisoned inside the stone, and now he was free. He reached out to touch the gem.

"My prison," he growled. "Hateful place—but perfect for the Overmind. Come here." Helaine did as he had ordered, and she felt his power reach out to envelop her. "Now," he ordered, "use your power of communications to download the Overmind from your chip into this jewel. I'll strengthen you, and place the binding spell on the stone so that the wretched creature can never get free."

Helaine could hardly wait to do as he said. It was getting harder and harder to focus her thoughts, but she managed to summon the strength and will to concentrate on the transfer.

The Overmind fought it, of course, but it had no chance at all. It was a creature of science, and here magic ruled supreme. Between her power and that of Nantor, the Overmind was quickly forced into the gemstone and then sealed inside it forever.

Helaine collapsed to the stone floor, exhausted, but with her mind once again her own. In a few moments, she'd have her strength back again. Already she could feel the magic starting to heal itself. The Diadem would be whole again soon, and magic would once more work properly.

Then her problems would *really* start.

She hadn't planned any further ahead than this. True, magic would heal, and the Diadem would recover. But she was here, trapped on Jewel, with Nantor. He was a lot stronger than she was, and he was hardly likely to want to share his impending reign over the Diadem with her—either as Helaine or as Eremin. The only thing keeping her alive right now was that he believed she was Eremin, and so had just as much power as he did. If he knew she was actually still Helaine, he was hardly likely to let her live.

"And now," Nantor said, laughing happily, "it's time to deal with you, girl." He reached out with his power, and slammed Helaine hard against the closest wall. "You're not Eremin, you silly little fool. Do you think I believe otherwise?"

"You *did*," Helaine gasped. She was completely drained of strength.

"Until we reached here," Nantor agreed. "But when we walked into this room, I *knew* you were lying." He gestured at the gemstones, all now spinning and giving off a wondrous light. "Eremin's gemstone was still alight—which meant that you had somehow resisted her taking control of your body. I didn't mind that, because I still needed you to restore the Analog. But you are not now needed. And I'm really glad that it's you in there, and not Eremin. I would have had to kill her, too, but that would have been far more difficult. Killing you, with your weak, contemptible power, will be so much simpler. And then I can go on to rule the Diadem all alone. And this time, there will be no world that will not fall to my power."

"What are you trying to do?" a familiar voice asked, mockingly. "Talk her to death?"

"Score!" Helaine felt a wonderful relief. "You're alive! And safe!"

"Well, I'd hardly call facing this maniac *safe*," Score answered, walking into the room. "But, yes, I'm here for you. You *always* seem to get in trouble, and need me to get you out of it."

Nantor scowled. "So, you managed to get off Earth somehow? Well, no matter—I would have had to hunt you down and kill you anyway. You've just saved me the trouble by coming here." He gathered up his magical energies. "The two of you will die, here and now—and it will from now on be only the One Who Rules!"

11

Pixel still wished that there were something he could do to help his friends, but he was virtually helpless. He could only observe as Nantor gathered power and threw a fireball toward Score and Helaine. Helaine was still crumpled against the wall, and unable to move, but Score somehow managed to step into the way and dissipate the blast.

"Is that the best that you can do?" Score mocked. "Don't forget, here on

Jewel, my own powers are far stronger—aided by the fact that you repaired the breach in magic, and everything's working fine again."

"It doesn't matter how much strength you've gained," Nantor snarled. "I have gained much, much more, and I know how to use it."

"We've *all* gained power," Score repeated, as he danced to one side, obviously luring Nantor away from attacking Helaine. She was still recovering from the attack on her. Pixel was puzzled—why was Score stressing that he had more power?

No! Pixel wished he could laugh, because the comment wasn't meant for Nantor, it was meant for *him.* And Score was right—he *did* have more strength again. Pixel couldn't take control of his body again, but he wasn't fading away as he had been. He could feel some strength returning, and he fought to keep alert. If Nantor let his guard down at all during this battle, then perhaps Pixel would have a chance to sabotage him and help Score.

Nantor realized none of this, of course. Partly that was because he was arrogant, but mostly it was because he didn't understand friendship and cooperation. He was used to being alone and thinking only of himself. With luck, it would never even occur to him that Pixel might attack him from inside his own mind.

Meanwhile, no matter how much bravado Score was displaying, he was in trouble. He was somehow managing not to get killed, but Nantor was certainly far stronger than him, and a lot more experienced at magic. Blast after blast exploded close to Score, and each time it seemed that Score's ability to protect himself was weakening. Nantor was having to be slightly careful—he didn't dare just blast the whole room, since that might damage the Diadem Analog—but he wasn't very restrained.

Still, Score's antics were producing one result that Pixel could see and Nantor couldn't: Nantor had almost forgotten Helaine's existence. Score was buying her time to recover, and Nantor hadn't worked this out. The oversight almost cost him the battle. He was rushing forward to strike again and again at Score with explosive blasts that were rattling the room. Suddenly, his legs were cut out from under him, and he fell, hard, to the stone floor. Pixel groaned with the pain that they both felt from the impact, as

Helaine rolled away and managed to get back to her feet.

"Thanks, Score," she said, panting slightly.

"Glad to be of help," Score said. "Anyway, I was having fun mocking this idiot. He really is a pompous jerk, isn't he?"

Why was Score still mocking Nantor? Pixel couldn't understand it. Surely Score knew that Nantor was bound to wear him down soon, even with Helaine to help out? Or was he attempting to distract Nantor so that Pixel could strike?

Pixel tried gently easing back into his own mind. Nantor's anger was consuming his attention, as he prepared to strike again at the ever-irritating Score. With his attention diverted, perhaps Pixel could start taking back his own body? Pixel knew he'd have to be very cautious about what he was doing . . .

"You two brats are no longer amusing," Nantor snapped.

"Ouch, that hurts," Score mocked. "I always wanted to be the comedian of the bunch. I guess that means you're applying for the job? In which case, here—have a custard pie." He materialized one and threw it at Nantor.

One swipe of the hand sent the pie smashing into the floor. "Stop making fun of me!" Nantor yelled, firing another blast.

"Touchy, isn't he?" Score asked Helaine, as they both dodged in different directions. The blast winded them, but did no other damage. "Do you think he has self-esteem problems?"

"I think he has many problems," Helaine said. "Right now, mostly us." She reached out with her magic, turning the stone under Nantor's feet into glue.

Furious, Nantor sent another fireball at the pair, and then focused on freeing his feet, and solidifying the ground again. "These minor irritations won't defeat me!" he yelled.

Pixel knew that he was right. But the distractions were buying Pixel time. He found that he could begin to take control of small functions in his body again. He made one finger wiggle, and even kept Nantor from being aware of it. He couldn't do very much at all, but perhaps Score wasn't planning on achieving a lot. Could it be that Score had something more in mind still?

"Maybe they won't," Score replied. "But if you keep this up, they might give you a heart attack. If you've still got a heart, of course."

Nantor was absolutely consumed now with a desire to hurt and kill Score. Score was right, Nantor *did* have emotional problems. He couldn't deal with frustration, and his anger was all-consuming. All he could focus on was making Score pay for his mockery.

And that, it turned out, was exactly what Score was after.

The next blast Nantor launched ripped through every last shred of Score's defenses. The explosion slammed him into the far wall, and he lay there, stunned, and unable to defend himself from further attacks. Pixel realized that Score had used all of his magical power to keep Nantor attacking him, and he had absolutely nothing left now.

"Time to die, you worm," Nantor snarled, readying a further attack.

Helaine stepped between them. She was limping slightly from her own injuries, but there was fury in her eyes. "You leave my boyfriend alone," she said, coldly.

"I'm not your boyfriend," Score protested, weakly.

"Shut up," Helaine said. "We'll discuss it later."

"There will *be* no later!" Nantor howled. "You are both dead!" He was ready now to launch the killer blast, and Pixel knew that his friends could not survive this. It was obviously time for him to act. He would have only one chance to stop Nantor, because as soon as the other realized what Pixel was doing, he would be able to focus on Pixel and stop him. He could only act while Nantor was distracted.

And then he saw the real reason for Score's actions. There was a blur of movement from the doorway. Score had managed to distract Nantor from looking behind him, and now Jenna was moving.

It all seemed so fast, that Pixel had virtually no time to understand what was happening before he acted. Nantor saw Jenna approaching, the hypodermic syringe ready in her hand. He started to turn and redirect his power to cut her down instead of Score.

No! Pixel would never allow any harm to come to Jenna! He reached now, with all of the strength he had left, and flooded Nantor's mind with every ounce of pain that he could. Nantor's vision swam and he screamed—and Jenna was there, pressing the needle into Nantor's arm. Pixel felt the plunger pressed, and the rush of liquid.

And then he felt nothing at all.

Pixel came back to consciousness slowly. He felt terrible, as if he'd stuck his fingers into an electrical socket and been burned. His head ached, and he wanted to throw up.

It was wonderful. He was back in his own body again, and there was no sign of Nantor!

Groaning, he opened his eyes and looked around. The first thing he saw was that he was still in the Analog room, and there was the sparkle of spinning gem stones in the background. Then he saw Jenna's sweet face, and the look of love and concern on it. He realized he was on the floor, but with his head in her lap.

"Can I stay here for a while?" he asked. "Two or three years should be enough."

Jenna bent down and kissed his nose. "Pixel, you're back," she breathed, happily.

"Yeah, and just as soppy as ever," Score complained. He limped into view. "Can't you forget about romance for a while and help us to clean up in here?"

Pixel struggled to sit up, but Jenna pushed him back down into her lap with no difficulty at all. "Score, you know he needs to rest. He's been through a lot."

"He wasn't the one getting his butt fried," Score complained. "In fact, I was really careful not to harm his body at all. Even though I could have been killed."

"Yes, we all know you're a real hero," Helaine growled. "Are you ever going to shut up about it?"

"No," Score said, smugly. "Especially not since my plan worked out perfectly, and yours screwed up halfway through."

"How can you say that?" Helaine yelled. "I fooled Nantor into thinking I was Eremin and got him to fix the Analog, didn't I?"

"A very clever plan, I might add," Pixel pointed out. "Don't ever believe you're not as smart as the rest of us again," he warned her. "That was great."

"But it would have gotten her killed," Score pointed out. "If I hadn't shown up, Nantor would have creamed her." He turned to Helaine. "Plans that get you killed are bad, got that?"

"Why do you care if I get killed or not?" Helaine asked him, glaring angrily. "You were even protesting that you weren't my boyfriend when Nantor was about to kill you!"

"Yeah, well, I was hoping you'd say I was again." Score looked rather ashamed of himself. "I kind of liked hearing it. And it's instinct, anyway. I'm a loner, you know."

"You're a fake," Jenna said kindly.

"Look, not to mess with the mood of triumph and all," Pixel said, "but will somebody explain to me what's happened? Where's Nantor? I can't feel him at all now."

"I'm not surprised," Jenna replied. She held up a small computer chip. "He's inside, and quite harmless."

Pixel touched his head. "Is that . . . ?"

"The one you had in there? Yes." Jenna smiled. "I had a powerful sedative in that injection I gave you. It knocked you and Nantor out cold. Then Helaine used her power of communication to force the unconscious Nantor's mind into this chip, and Score and I together removed it from your head. Now he's trapped in here, and won't ever get free again. With no chip in your head, he can't take over your mind ever again."

"Which reminds me," Helaine said. "I still have a chip in *my* head." She turned to Score and bowed her head. "Get it out."

"See what I mean?" Score complained. "Always giving orders." He bent to focus his magic. "Okay, your snootiness—it's all gone. Happy now, or do you have more orders for me?"

"Just one," Helaine growled. "Bend down a bit." When he did, she kissed him on the lips. "Thank you. I *hated* having that in there."

Score looked so surprised that he didn't even manage a sarcastic remark. It looked as if he'd enjoyed the kiss.

"Okay," Pixel said. His strength was almost returned now, mostly thanks to the huge flow of power about them. "So the Three Who Rule are imprisoned. The Diadem is safe, and we're all in reasonable health. Does that mean that everything is okay again?"

"Not quite," Jenna answered. "We still have a couple of really big problems left. Are you up to traveling?"

Pixel rose to his feet, a little shakily. He didn't mind at all when she placed an arm around his waist to help support him. "Where are we going?"

"First of all, back to Calomir," Jenna said. "There's a few things to clear up there." She led the way from the Analog Room. A subdued Score closed the door, and then sealed it again with the unicorn horn. Jenna concentrated, and a portal opened in front of them.

"I won't miss this place," Pixel commented. "It always seems to mean serious trouble." With a little help from Jenna, he stepped through the portal, and back to the planet of his birth.

12

Jenna was surrounded by blue-skinned people with guns pointed at her as she emerged from the portal.

"Right," Fargo growled, as Score and Helaine were the last to emerge. "What is the password?"

"Oh, right." Score slapped his forehead. "Me and my plans." he had to think for a second. "Template."

The guns were slowly lowered, and Fargo managed a smile. "Everything worked out, then?" she asked.

"Yes," Pixel answered. "The Overmind is gone forever. Nantor and the Three won't be back." He glanced around the hospital. "But there's still lot to do, isn't there? How are you coping?"

"We're barely managing," Fargo said, honestly. "Your friends Byte and Dayta are rounding up the kids as they emerge from the Houses. Without the Overmind's control, all the computers have stopped working. About a third of the population is probably comatose, and there's not much chance of them ever recovering. Everyone is confused, food supplies will be a problem, and just getting some sort of order going will be chaos." Then she grinned. "But our minds are our own, and our future is up to us, and not the computers. So there's good and bad."

"Like most of life," Jenna said.

"Yes." Fargo sighed. "I don't know what we'd have done without your help," she said, honestly. "We'd all still be slaves. For a bunch of kids, you're very effective revolutionaries."

"We never aimed to be," Pixel said. "All we wanted to do was to come and visit my parents. And we never did find them."

"It might still be possible," Score said. "I mean, there's always DNA testing, and so forth."

Helaine punched his arm. "Or he could just use his ruby," she pointed out. "Magic could show them to him." She studied Pixel.

It was obviously a struggle for him to reach a decision, but eventually he shook his head. "The chances are that they're either dead or brain-dead," he said. "And I really wouldn't want to see them as zombies. Besides, thanks to the Overmind, whoever my birth parents were, they never knew me. The ones I have memories of are just creations of that demented computer program. So what I thought I came here to find doesn't exist." He reached out a hand to Fargo. "But there's a wonderful promise for a future now."

Jenna hesitated, knowing she had to say what was on her mind, but worried about the answer she'd get. "Do you want to stay here?" she asked. "This is your home world, after all, and these are your folks. They've got a world to rebuild, and I'll bet they would appreciate your help."

Pixel looked at Fargo, who nodded. "We'd be really glad to have you here," she said. "All of you. We do need a lot of help, and you four would probably make great administrators."

Score threw his hands up. "Why is it that everybody seems to assume we want to take charge of things?" he complained. "Look, lady, I appreciate the offer, but I'm really *way* too lazy to make any kind of decent administrator."

"That's true enough," Helaine agreed. "And I don't think I should be trusted with power. It might make me selfish and nasty." She glared at Score. "And if you say that it's too late, I'll flatten you."

"I never said a word," Score protested.

"Then maybe there's hope for you yet," Helaine said.

Jenna looked at Pixel. If he wanted to stay, she could understand it. But what did he want?

Pixel looked at her. "Jenna, how about you?" he asked. That was typical, that he would think of her first.

"I'd be happy to help if I can," she said, slowly. "But I don't know if I could stay here. I really understand so little of science, and this world teems with it. I'd feel very inadequate here."

"You would never be inadequate anywhere," he told her, hugging her. "You'll always be outstanding."

"If you wish to stay, then, I will stay with you," she promised him. "As long as I'm with you, I'll be happy."

Pixel gave her a quick kiss, ignoring the gagging noises coming from Score's direction. Then he turned to Fargo. "I'll be happy to help," he said. "But this is no longer my home. If there's one thing that my adventures have taught me, it's that there is a lot to do everywhere, and not just here. I've experienced so much since I left Calomir, and I've been able to help a lot of people. Staying here on one world would be kind of . . . limiting. But it will always be my home, and I will be back to see how things are going. Can you understand?"

Fargo nodded and hugged him. "Yes, of course. And you're right—it would be selfish of us to keep you here when there are other worlds out there that could use your aid." She looked like she was fighting back tears as she glanced about the group. "Before you came, I was certain that life was hopeless, that I was doomed to live and die a slave. You all taught me that I was wrong. You gave me hope, and then you gave us all a future. Thank you."

"Let's get out of here," Score muttered, "before she tries adopting us, or giving us medals, or something." Helaine punched him gently on the arm.

"We do have a few other things to do," Jenna said. "We will be back, and do what we can. But at the moment, we have a very important job to do."

"More work?" Score complained. "Can't we just take a vacation? I need to lie back and do nothing."

"That's your normal life," Helaine replied.

"I know, and I miss it."

Jenna ignored their bickering, knowing that it covered their affection for each other—and knowing that both of them knew this also. She formed another portal, and looked around. "Time to go," she said. They waved their goodbyes, and then left Calomir and its people to their work of building a new society.

Jenna emerged back in Shanara's den. The magician was there, waiting nervously. Oracle hovered in the background. Blink was dozing on the nearest table, on a pile of books. As the portal closed behind them, Jenna looked around at the five tense faces.

"We have to deal with this," she said, firmly. "Shanara and Oracle set a trap for the three of you, a trap that was intended to kill you. Unless we can get past this, none of us will be able to trust the others again." Nobody seemed to want to start talking, and she understood how difficult this had to be for all of them.

"Score, you were the one most affected. What do you have to say about it?"

Score shuffled uncomfortably. Then he sighed and looked up. "I almost died," he said. He looked over at Shanara. "I can't just forget that. But . . . well, having seen what you look like, and knowing that Traxis did it to you . . . I can't entirely blame you. In your place, I'd have probably done something like what you did."

"It was the hardest decision of my life," Shanara said in a low, breaking voice. "I truly did not want to harm any of you. But we simply couldn't allow the Three ever to return. You have no idea how bad they were."

"Actually," Pixel said, gently, "I have a *very* good idea. I had to share a brain with Nantor, remember? And I saw just how selfish, callous and evil he was. I was prepared to kill myself to stop him from ever living again, if I could only have thought of some way to do it. So I guess I'm kind of on your side, at least a little."

Oracle stepped forward. "And it was mainly my fault," he said, able to speak normally once more now that the magic was restored. "I had to twist Shanara's arm into agreeing."

157

"That would have been something to see," Score commented. "How'd you manage that grip?"

"You know what I mean." Oracle bowed his head in shame. "I was a servant of the Three for many years. I was forced to carry their threats and demands to many people. I saw them commit many atrocities. I couldn't bear for those times to ever return again."

"We get the point already," Score complained. "Three Who Rule, bad. Want them back, never you do. Now can we just change the subject?"

"Not quite," Jenna said. "There's one more thing first." She could feel the excess magic dancing through her system from her stay on Jewel. She was in no danger of burning out, but it had to go *somewhere*, and there was a very obvious place. "Shanara—please, drop your illusion."

Shanara paled. "Jenna, this is very hard for me," she said. "I know you and Score have seen what I'm *really* like, but . . ."

"You have to trust me on this," Jenna said gently. "I do not ask it lightly of you. I do know what it means to you. But you *must* drop your illusion."

The magician swallowed and hesitated. Then she abruptly nodded, and allowed the image covering her scarred form to fall away. Helaine and Pixel gasped in shock, and even Jenna and Score groaned at the sight.

With her power of healing, increased by the magic boost she had gained on Jewel, Jenna reached out. As the power flowed, she could almost *feel* the scars and the broken, misshappen bones mending. The drain on her was enormous, but she refused to stop, or to even slow down. She poured her energies into healing.

Shanara gave a gasp as her body glowed in health and strength. The scars started to heal, the knots in her bones straightened. Her skin was restored to its glowing condition.

After moments, after an eternity, Jenna almost collapsed. Helaine's strong arm supported her, and they all looked at Shanara.

She looked much as she always did, though her hair was a fairly common golden color. But she was bright and refreshed, and astonished. "I feel so different," she breathed.

"The power of healing," Jenna said. "You are what you were before Traxis got hold of you."

"A real babe," Score said, approvingly. Aware that Helaine was glaring at him, he added: "Not that you're exactly ugly, or anything. Quite the opposite, in fact—you're a knock-out." Almost under his breath, he added, "In more ways than one."

Oracle raised an eyebrow, and looked at Pixel. "Did that mean what I thought it meant?"

"Yes." Pixel nodded. "They've finally admitted that they like one another. They even kissed."

"It's about time," Oracle said.

"What is this, a dating service?" Score complained. "We'll kiss if we feel like it. And we'll fight if we feel like it, okay?"

"Whatever," Pixel said, grinning.

Score scowled as he looked at Shanara again. "You know, the more I look at you, the more it seems like I know you."

"Score," Helaine growled, "you've known her for ages. And I'd appreciate it if you didn't look at her quite like that."

Shanara smiled gently. "But he *is* right," she said. "He *does* know me, because he once loved me more than anyone else."

Score groaned, and covered his face, "Ouch!" he complained. "I knew it. You said that Traxis had been chosen to hurt you because he should have loved you the most. You two were married, weren't you? You might have been my wife, right?" He looked scared of the answer, and Jenna knew why—if Shanara was once Traxis's wife, that would certainly complicate his growing relationship with Helaine.

Shanara laughed in delight. "Oh, Score," she said. "You always were so over-dramatic. No, I'm not your once and future wife, you idiot. I'm your mother."

YA   Peel, John
DIADEM   Book of Doom

7/22/08 $4.99